More Praise for

SAY NICE THINGS ABOUT DETROIT

"Lasser . . . composes his sympathetic cast into tableaux that are meaningful, even emblematic. . . . His restrained portrait of Detroit evokes real pathos."
—*Publishers Weekly*, starred review

"By the end we get to know the city almost as intimately as we know the characters." —*Kirkus Reviews*

"Readers will savor this fast-paced tale of redemption in one sitting." —*Library Journal*

"In prose as sparse as the streets of the modern Motor City, *Say Nice Things About Detroit* captures the hopelessness and determination underpinning a blighted city unraveled by racism." —*Jewish Book Council*

"Lasser's narrative is rich in detail about Detroit geography, weather, music and racial politics, and has an authenticity that's hard to match."   —*Detroit News*

"Mr. Lasser is a fine storyteller and his easy, understated style moves the novel along."   —*Washington Times*

"You'll love Scott Lasser's style. His book spans a few years but keeps moving with dialogue that's natural and alive: whites and blacks in Detroit, a setting you come to know and can feel what it's about. I know; I've been here most of my life."   —Elmore Leonard

"This is a sharp, clear portrait of who we are now. Scott Lasser continues to shape a very distinct literary map."   —Colum McCann

"Scott Lasser has written a moving story of people whose lives are stalled until they face events and places they'd rather avoid. His book suggests that for people and cities, life's greatest rewards are only achieved through struggle. A moving tribute to second chances and the august, desolate, melancholy city of Detroit."   —Thomas McGuane

"In a city famous for ruin, a pilgrim's tale of rebirth and renewal: Scott Lasser's narrative gifts are abundant, his characters a compelling and convincing lot. *Say Nice Things About Detroit*, while true to life's damages and sadnesses, is nonetheless a joyous, vital read."

—Thomas Lynch

"*Say Nice Things About Detroit*, Scott Lasser's new novel, is a moving, fast-paced, economical story of race, crime, and hope. Weighted by the death of his son and the end of his marriage, David Halpert, a young lawyer, returns home to the chaos of a dying Detroit to discover a love affair and his own brush with violence as the book rushes to its stunning conclusion."—Susan Richards Shreve

also by Scott Lasser

THE YEAR THAT FOLLOWS

ALL I COULD GET

BATTLE CREEK

SAY NICE THINGS ABOUT DETROIT

Scott Lasser

W. W. Norton & Company

NEW YORK • LONDON

For information about permission to reproduce selections from this
book, write to Permissions, W. W. Norton & Company, Inc.,
500 Fifth Avenue, New York, NY 10110

For information about special discounts for bulk purchases,
please contact W. W. Norton Special Sales at
specialsales@wwnorton.com or 800-233-4830

Manufacturing by RR Donnelley, Harrisonburg
Book design by Fearn Cutler de Vicq
Production manager: Devon Zahn

Library of Congress Cataloging-in-Publication Data

Lasser, Scott.
Say nice things about Detroit / Scott Lasser. — 1st ed.
p. cm.
ISBN 978-0-393-08299-9
1. Life change events—Fiction. 2. Homecoming—Fiction.
3. Murder—Investigation—Fiction. 4. Detroit Metropolitan
Area (Mich.)—Social conditions—21st century—Fiction.
5. Detroit (Mich.)—Economic conditions—21st century—Fiction.
6. Detroit (Mich.)—Race relations—Fiction. I. Title.
PS3562.A7528S29 2012
813'.54—dc23
2012006784

ISBN 978-0-393-34553-7 pbk.

W. W. Norton & Company, Inc.
500 Fifth Avenue, New York, N.Y. 10110
www.wwnorton.com

W. W. Norton & Company Ltd.
Castle House, 75/76 Wells Street, London W1T 3QT

1 2 3 4 5 6 7 8 9 0

For Pam

You think of Detroit in the modern period as a huge, vast African-American ghetto. It's like New Orleans after the flood. Detroit has been through all this and they didn't even have a natural disaster. It just got washed over by America.

—John Sinclair

I don't mean to be sarcastic, but there just isn't anyone left to kill.

—Stanley Christmas, Detroit mayoral candidate, on the 14 percent drop in the murder rate

2006

I

They fled. Tom Phillips to Orlando, Brady Johnson to Dallas, Jeff Lombardo to Chicago, Tim Forrester to L.A. David couldn't think of a single friend from high school who still lived in Detroit, or anywhere near it. David himself had moved to Denver, but now he was back.

It was the very first morning of his return that he noticed the photos, a light-skinned black man and a blond woman, side-by-side in the *Free Press*, front page and above the fold. Recognition came slowly, then suddenly. He took the paper and sat down to study it. Three nights ago these two had been gunned down in an E-Class Mercedes just north of Greektown, a dozen shots fired at close range. The paper identified the male victim, Dirk Burton, as a retired FBI agent. The woman was Natalie Brooks. The paper speculated on what they were doing in a place and car like that, on whether the killing was racial, which was doubted by a police source, who said violence against interracial couples tended not to happen in black neighborhoods. Perhaps the cops didn't yet know they were brother and sister.

David dated Natalie in high school, a two-year affair that fell apart when they went to different colleges. Natalie was the serious love of his youth, maybe his life, unforgettable still. Evans was the family name. David recalled when as a teenager he pulled his Chevy into the Evanses' driveway and parked behind a large black Mercedes with fat wheels and tinted windows. Natalie walked out of the house with a black man, tall and broad-shouldered. He moved with an athlete's swagger. "This is my brother, Dirk," Natalie said.

David had known Natalie since she was fourteen, and there had never been mention of a brother, black or otherwise. The Evans sisters were blond; they would have been considered fair in Sweden. In the milky summer light, on the edge of adulthood, David sensed that there was an awful lot going on in the world he had no idea about. He learned that Natalie, her sister, Carolyn, and Dirk shared the same mother, Tina, a German immigrant who'd made her way to Detroit in the fifties. Later, Natalie related the story of Dirk's birth: rushed to the hospital when her water broke, Tina was wheeled from the white ward to the black when the father showed up. Then, as now, half white was black.

It was the one time David met Dirk. He showed David the Mercedes; they leaned into the car through opposite doors, their heads together in front of the German sound system. The vehicle, seized from a drug dealer and pushed into service for Dirk's undercover work, was more expensive portable stereo system than automobile. "You can't believe the shit these dopers spend money on," Dirk said. Then he turned up the bass till the vibrations made David's sternum hum.

Dirk looked a little older in the newspaper photo (it had been twenty-five years), his hair now shaved down to stubble. Natalie was still beautiful, blond and angular. It was hard to think of them as dead. Natalie especially. It was as if his youth had died with her.

·   ·   ·

SIX WEEKS HAD passed since his father called. "It's your mother," the old man said. She was forgetting things; often she became disoriented, so much so that he could no longer let her drive. She was belligerent. She swore often.

"Mom?" David asked.

"A blue streak. You can't believe the things that come out of her mouth."

David asked what the doctors thought.

"Dementia. Wonderful, huh? Like I can't tell that myself. These doctors are no help. There's no cure, just some precautionary things you can do."

"Like what?"

"Lock her in the house, so she doesn't wander outside in her housecoat. Still, she can get out. I'm always on guard."

"Jeez, Dad."

"Jesus, hey-ZEUS, Yahveh, Allah. Pick any damn god you want. It won't help."

David sighed.

"I need you to come home," his father said.

"To Detroit?"

"Yes, of course."

"Okay. I'll visit."

"Not just for a visit. I need you to come and stay."

"Stay?" David asked. Only the demented moved to Detroit; his father had to know this. "Why?"

"Because I don't know what to do."

*　*　*

At first David resisted the idea. He was sitting in his office, looking out through the haze to the tawny foothills of the Rocky Mountains, when he decided there was nothing important holding him to Denver, or anywhere. He was three years a partner at Cornish and Kohl, a position not nearly as lucrative as he had hoped. He specialized in estate planning and asset protection. "Well," his father said, "people are always dying, and the asset-protection side of things must mean you're protecting people from other lawyers." Solomon Halpert had worked his entire life in manufacturing—for him the only worthy profession, other than perhaps medicine—and this was as close to an endorsement as David was going to get. Despite the subject of David's work, it never seemed life-or-death; he didn't see how three months off would leave anyone in the lurch.

He rented an apartment in the suburb of Birmingham, not far from his parents' house. His father had been slow to give up on the city proper, even after '67, but move he did, first to Oak Park (three miles north of 8 Mile Road, the green line with the city proper) and then out to Maple (15 Mile) before David reached high school. David's room was still intact in that house. His mother had taken down the Led Zeppelin poster, and the one of the Lange Girl ("Soft Inside"), but it was otherwise the same, twin bed and bookshelves with paperback copies of *The Hobbit*, *Paper Lion*, and other books of his youth. It was a museum, that room; he couldn't stay there. Duty was one thing, but he could only go so far. Besides, he suspected his father wanted him close, but not that close.

• • •

"YOUR FATHER THINKS I've lost my mind," his mother told him when he walked in the door. No hello, even. She hugged him, pronounced him too thin, and told him she'd fix him a drink. She was still a trim woman, small, her hair cut short and dyed shoe-polish black.

"Are you?" he asked.

"Am I what?" she said.

"Losing your mind."

"Not yet." She looked back at his father. "But he's pushing me."

David stuck his hand out, but his father bypassed it and hugged him. The man was a former marine, and not a hugger. "Thank you," he whispered in David's ear. His mother, meanwhile, was making drinks at the bar. "She insisted on cooking," his father whispered.

"So?"

"You'll see."

The house had the same framed prints from the Galerie Maeght, the same black upright Steinway, unmoved for three decades. His parents didn't play but had bought the piano for David, then forced him to take lessons because his mother had read that studying music was good for a student's math scores. She probably figured that if she didn't get a scientist she'd get a concert pianist, rather than neither.

She handed him a scotch. As a kid he couldn't stand the smell; now he drank it only at home, for medicinal purposes.

"So tell me," she said, "how's Julie?"

The ex-wife, back in Boston now. He hadn't talked to her in two and a half years. He was glad to be free of her, and yet it still hurt like hell.

"Good," he said.

"Tell her I said hello. You should marry that girl, you know."

He looked at his father, who stared back, then nodded just slightly.

"Mom, I did marry her."

She studied him. "Oh," she said at last. She looked away,

perhaps remembering, perhaps not, and then retreated to the kitchen.

．　．　．

LATER, HIS MOTHER went up to get ready for bed. Dinner had been excruciating. She'd made pasta but drained it too soon, so that each bite was a deafening crunch. She hadn't washed the lettuce; on his first and only bite of salad he found himself chewing dirt. Again, it was terribly loud. His mother asked him ludicrous questions—"How are your grades?"—and, worst of all, she wanted to know about Cory, her one grandson, dead now more than four years.

He was a man divided against himself, burning with undying love for his dead child and at the same time wanting to forget, to put the whole thing out of his mind, to be nothing more than a new person, a man without a past. Tough in your parents' house.

Cory would have been sixteen this year, but four years ago he'd gone skiing with his friend Jess Barker and Jess's brother and mother and father. Coming out of the mountains on a snowy night, Jess's father called from I-70 to say they were in Georgetown, moving now; they'd be there in maybe an hour. But then the traffic stopped and a semi ran into them, killing the Barker family whole and destroying the Halperts just the same.

David calculated that the accident happened maybe twenty minutes after he'd talked to Lance Barker; for almost two hours he was oblivious of the disaster. Then he called and got voicemail. Forty minutes later he saw the accident report on Channel 9. Still, he didn't make the connection. That came later, when he called the state police, who took his name and number and then sent a trooper to his door. Snow collected on the plastic that covered the trooper's flat-brimmed hat. The man wore a look so grim that David understood immediately, looking at this stranger, a picture of bad news.

. . .

"YOU SEE WHAT I'm talking about?" His father handed David another Johnnie Walker Black, the smell of home.

David nodded.

"Sometimes I find her sitting on the bed, crying. When I ask what's wrong, she says she doesn't know what she's doing."

David studied his father, who had fought in Korea, then spent three years in Japan before returning to work for Bethlehem Steel. Deep vertical lines divided his cheeks. His eyebrows had grown bushy. Unlike David, he had all of his hair, a lot of it dark for a man of seventy-four.

"I've talked to her about it," he said.

"About the forgetting?" David asked.

"About the home." His father had put her on the waiting list for a place in Orchard Lake, a fine institution, he said, with locked, coded doors, so she couldn't wander away.

"Are you sure?" David asked.

"Unless you think you can look after her. And believe

me, you have no idea what that entails. Sometimes—" His father stopped talking. He waved his hand, as if to say, *Never mind.*

"What?"

He shook his head, but spoke anyway.

"Sometimes she wets the bed. Or she forgets to get up and go to the bathroom. I have her in diapers now. Your mother. She was something once."

*   *   *

IT FELT GOOD to be out of Denver. In coming back to Detroit, it was as if he were skirting his bad times, going back before they happened. David's apartment sat walking distance from Birmingham's commercial core; it was a clean, furnished ground-floor one-bedroom rented easily for three months, so happy was the landlord to fill a vacancy. David liked the idea of walking, of not having to get in a car (very un-Detroit) to buy a sandwich. His folks' house was a mile away, close enough to walk if he wanted.

A few evenings into his return the newspaper with Dirk's and Natalie's picture still lay on the kitchen counter. He found an old phone book and located the Evanses' number. It was too late to call, so he wrote the number out and left it on the Formica countertop.

He wondered what his father would do when his mother went into the home. David resolved to take him on excursions. They could revisit all the old sites—the Henry Ford Museum and Greenfield Village, Greektown, the DIA, the

Ren Cen, Belle Isle—just as they'd done when David was a boy. He thought of these places, embedded in his memory, and felt he was considering ruins. But no, they had to be there still; it hadn't been that long. He vowed to see them all; perhaps bearing witness would preserve them.

He decided to take a walk. It was a warm and humid evening. He strolled down Merrill Street, past the Varsity Shop, the one landmark he remembered, where his father used to buy him cleats, baseball gloves, his first cup. The year his Little League team won the championship the team photo went up on the wall, and it stayed there for a year, till it was taken down to make way for newer champions.

He continued on. The shops were all closed for the night, but Birmingham maintained its sheen of prosperity. He felt possessed with an odd feeling of well-being, walking the streets that he'd known as a teenager. He could hear traffic nearby on Woodward. The air had become damp, portending rain; there was a far-off sound of electrical disturbance, the thunder a low rumble, big guns in the distance. He walked on, confident, as if things here might work out right.

II

HER MOTHER SLEPT, sedated, unable to function without a drug of some sort. Last night Carolyn had helped her with the child-resistant top of the prescription bottle, tapped out two yellow pills as instructed, remembering the time long ago when her mother had given her children's aspirin, little orange tablets, or antibiotics prescribed by her father. Carolyn's mother believed in pills and their life-changing qualities, even if the change was nothing more than a good night's sleep.

Natalie was dead. Dirk was dead. The Bureau was evasive, either reluctant to divulge details or not in possession of them. The one thing Carolyn knew was that Dirk had not been lost. He knew the city, the white areas as well as the black, and especially the dangerous parts, the "Klingon air space," as he called them, where he'd worked undercover (drugs, guns, you name it) for the better part of two decades. "Not that Bloomfield Hills or Grosse Pointe are necessarily easier," he once told her. "At least for me." He gave up the undercover work when he turned forty, saying it was a young man's game, and too dangerous. That was more than ten years ago. The Mercedes he died in was his own; he'd developed a taste for them.

Carolyn was home, but this wasn't really home. Her mother had sold their house when Carolyn's father died and moved to this townhome, where she paid a monthly fee and someone else did the maintenance and groundskeeping, chores which had once been the province of Carolyn's father, Arthur. He was English by birth, trained at Johns Hopkins, an immigrant like her mother, but also different. Perhaps being English made him as forbidden as Dirk's father. It was hard to think of your mother in rebellion, but she'd left Germany, come to America, married a black man, then an Englishman. Something must have been going on.

• • •

TINA STAGGERED INTO the kitchen a little after ten; she'd gone to bed the night before at nine. Carolyn watched as she heaped two teaspoons of sugar into a demitasse of coffee, then added cream. Real cream. Old World all the way. She waited for her mother to sit, exchanged a couple of pleasantries, and then asked, "Mom, you came all the way from Germany—why did you pick Detroit?"

"Back then," her mother said, "Detroit was a very prosperous place. One of the most prosperous in the world."

"Detroit?"

"Sure. Besides, I was nineteen. I had a friend I met in New York, Trudy Schembler, also German. She said there was plenty of money in Detroit. Lots of Germans also. So we came. I didn't like New York. I came from a small town. New York was . . . pfft. Crazy. Too many people."

"And you thought Detroit was a small town?" Carolyn asked.

"What did I know?"

Carolyn walked to the counter and poured herself more coffee.

"How old are you now? Forty-seven?" her mother asked.

"Thanks, Mom. Forty-two."

"You look good. You've taken care of yourself. How's my grandson?"

"Pretty full of himself, actually."

"Why don't you bring him to visit me?"

"Mom, why don't you come to us? I have a job. Marty has a job. Kevin's in school. We're three and you're—" She stopped herself. *Oh, God,* she thought. She hadn't seen Dirk and Natalie in over a year, and now she would never see them. She looked at her mother, who was carefully sipping her coffee, her blond hair (dyed now) helter-skelter on her head. *You're alone,* Carolyn thought, but she didn't say it, and that was okay, because her mother was always happy with a little silence. She thought of Kevin and the impossibility of losing him, the horror of losing a child; her mother had lost two and there were simply no words for that. Silence would have to do.

.   .   .

THE FUNERAL HAD taken place two days before, Catholic per her mother's wishes. When Carolyn tried to count the times she'd been to church, other than for weddings and funerals, she couldn't get to five. At the cemetery the bodies were buried next to each other, beside Arthur. Their mother's plot was there, too. Very German, Carolyn thought, to have a plan like that right to the end.

The funeral took place on a warm day, the leaves on the beech and several oaks full and fluttering. Carolyn stood

23

by her mother. It seemed that almost half the crowd was dark-suited men, FBI agents, more men than she would have guessed her brother knew, though she didn't know Dirk that well; they didn't have the same father and had never even lived in the same house, didn't come from the same neighborhood, had only this odd connection of German blood. She reached over and touched her mother's arm.

At the end of the service she and her mother threw dirt on the graves. Carolyn felt the finality of it then. The priest held her as she sobbed. It had always been up to her to be the stoic one, the responsible one, though what she'd done was to run as far away from her family as she could get. Now Dirk and Natalie were dead. It felt as if she'd had some hand in it, as if by her absence she had allowed it to happen.

. . .

SHE WAITED TILL almost eleven, then called Marty on his cell, knowing he'd be driving Kevin to camp. It was only eight there, probably cooler than a summer day in Michigan, though it would stay that same lovely temperature for months. It never really got cold. If there was anything she missed about Detroit it was the fall, the special smell the air got as the leaves came alight, then fell. "Football weather," it was called, a phrase that had no meaning in southern California.

"Hey," Marty said. "How's it going?"

"Great," she said. Marty and Kevin had flown back

home for work and camp the day after the funeral. Carolyn planned to stay on—"Ten days or so," she told Marty—to see her mother through.

"It couldn't even be good," Marty said. He'd warned her she wouldn't make the week and a half, but then again, he'd never much liked her mother, a sentiment that was returned. "He lacks a deep soul," her mother had warned her before the marriage, but Carolyn had ignored this, as she did all her mother's warnings.

She asked to talk to Kevin.

"Hey, Mom," the boy said. She was reminded of the Bluetooth, that the boy could hear everything.

"How's camp?"

"Fine."

"Doing anything special?" She waited for the reply, but the call had been dropped. This was how it was in the cell age; so many conversations ended without a goodbye.

* * *

BACK IN THE kitchen, her mother was still sitting at the table in her bathrobe, making no attempt to get up or even read the paper. Carolyn asked her if she wanted to go for a drive.

"No, but you go. I'll be fine."

"It would do you good to get out," Carolyn said.

"I don't think so."

Carolyn considered whether to counter this challenge

and decided against it. She could pretend her mother was always right until she went home to California.

The day was bleached white, a high, bright cloud layer seeming to make everything fuzzy. The rental car was a Mazda—unfathomable in the old days, a rental agency in Detroit renting a Japanese model—and she drove it down Telegraph. Her knowledge of the area had faded; she'd left at eighteen for good. She decided to go to Hancock Street to see the place where her brother and sister died. She thought she might be able to move on better if she could see the spot. She hadn't seen Natalie in almost two years, not since she and Marty had bought Natalie a plane ticket to L.A. On that trip they'd promised to stay in better touch, but it hadn't happened. Carolyn should have made more effort, and now she wouldn't get the chance.

She crossed Maple, past the old Machus Red Fox, a different restaurant now but still the same building, a kind of memorial to Jimmy Hoffa. His disappearance was part of her history, another big milestone along the route of Detroit's demise. Close to 12 Mile she exited Telegraph to the right—the car dealers were still here, though now you could buy a Nissan or Toyota, Saab or Volvo, and no one would shout at you or take a sledgehammer to the vehicle while you waited at a red light—and then followed the entrance ramp, first right and then left as the road curved south and east into the city. She felt conscious of her breathing, deep and a little rapid, as she was driving seventy-two in the right-hand lane, past the retaining walls, shredded tires, and trash, a splintered crib, on the shoulder. The seat beside her held a copy of the police report and a MapQuest printout. She flicked down the automatic door locks and drove on.

She took the Lodge too far, then, realizing it, exited by the river, turning on a street called Randolph, then Gratiot. Soon she was skirting around the new Ford Field and Comerica Park (no more Tiger Stadium in Detroit). She headed back west to Woodward, then Hancock, the street on the report. Not much beauty here, but nothing sinister, just old and empty buildings under the drab sky, a sheet of newspaper cartwheeling down the street, crabgrass growing out of the sidewalks, not a person on them, an empty city street on a completely normal day.

She approached Cass and the parking lot near the murder spot. Police lights flashed red and blue behind her. She eased the car to the right with two hands on the wheel, ten o'clock and two o'clock, just as she'd been taught as a teenager. The cruiser pulled in behind her.

The cop and his partner sat in their car a long time; she waited, wondering what she'd done wrong. She hadn't been speeding; she was sure of that. She had her license, assumed the registration and proof of insurance were in the glovebox. A second police car pulled up. The first policeman got out, walked to her window, and asked for her license, registration, and proof of insurance.

He studied the California license for a long time.

"What are you doing here?" he asked finally. He was a

large, middle-aged man with a bit of a paunch, evident as he stood at her window. His skin was the deep, rich color of stained maple.

"I'm trying to get to the corner of Hancock and Cass," she said.

The cop looked to his left. Her destination was less than half a block away. "Why?"

"My brother and sister died there," she said.

"You're saying that the FBI agent, Burton, was your brother?"

"Same mother," she explained. It always needed explanation.

He waved the other cop car away, then handed her back her license and the other paperwork, which the rental car company had packed up in a plastic zip-lock baggie.

"Drive up to Cass," he told her. "Turn right, put your car in the lot. We'll stay with you. I don't want you out here alone."

The cop's partner was another black man, older, his hair mixed with gray, frosty curls. She liked these men immediately. They meant to protect her.

"It's the middle of the day," she said.

"You got the art museum just a couple blocks north, Wayne State's nearby, but you shouldn't come down here alone. Not a woman, especially not a blond woman."

"You're asking for trouble," the older cop said. "Even if it ain't bad trouble."

Soon she was standing with the two men at the corner.

"How did this happen?" she asked.

"I wouldn't park here at night," the older cop said. "No way."

"He was waiting for someone," said the other.

"And vice versa, it looks like."

A thought came to her. "Why did you pull me over?" she asked.

"You looked lost."

"What's that mean?"

"A white woman in a rental car driving slow around here? That's lost."

"Maybe looking for the art museum," said the older cop.

A moment passed, as if to accentuate the basic insincerity of what they were saying.

"You thought I was here to score," Carolyn said. "You racial-profiled me."

"Whoa, ma'am," said the younger cop. "None a that. You looked lost. We were just trying to help." He paused. "Protect and serve. That's what this is all about, ma'am."

"Would you have stopped a black woman here?"

"A black woman would have been speeding," he said.

III

THE *FREE PRESS* divulged that the victims were brother and sister, and for a couple days the story moved the mayor's troubles below the fold. David paced back and forth in front of his kitchen counter, looking at the phone number. He wanted to have an idea what to say; he was bad at speaking on the fly. There was a reason he hadn't tried to be a litigator. He considered himself especially bad on the phone and often practiced how he thought the conversation might go. *Mrs. Evans, this is David Halpert calling. I read about Dirk and Natalie in the papers. I am so sorry. It's horrible.*

He felt an obligation to make the call, but he dreaded it. It was the sorrow. He'd had enough with sorrow. He could let his life become an exercise in it—his son, his marriage, his mother, eventually his father, his city—or he could make it otherwise. Cory was dead four years now. Simply to choose to live differently made as much sense as anything.

He picked up the phone and dialed the Evanses, seven digits. He got an error message. The phone company wanted him to use the new area code.

A woman answered.

"Is this Mrs. Evans?"

"Put me on your do-not-call list," she said.

"Mrs. Evans, it's David Halpert calling."

A pause. "David? Natalie's friend?"

"Yes. I happen to be in town and, well, I've seen the papers and so I'm calling to say I'm very, very sorry. I don't—"

"Thank you, David," she said, saving him. "How are you doing?"

"I'm fine."

"And your parents?"

"My dad is good. My mom, she's having some medical issues."

"You give them my best."

"I will," he said.

"Would you like to speak to Carolyn?" she asked.

"Why, yes, sure," he said, for no other reason than he didn't want to say no to Mrs. Evans, nor did he want to talk to her any longer. Carolyn? He'd last seen her when she was sixteen. What would he say to her?

"David?"

"Hi, Carolyn."

"Do you actually live here?"

They spent several minutes catching up. She lived in Los Angeles with her husband and son.

"I think I'd heard you were in Arizona, right?"

"Denver. But I'm staying a few months, to help my dad with my mom. She's losing it. Some kind of dementia."

"That's too bad."

"I'm sorry about Natalie. And Dirk. God, I don't know what to say."

"You've said it," she answered. A long, uncomfortable silence followed before Carolyn spoke again. "My sister still talked about you every once in a while."

"I'm surprised to hear that," he said.

"Well, you shouldn't be. I don't think she ever got over the lack of that goodbye."

"I don't know that I did, either," he said. Natalie's parents had taken her off to school early. Natalie had called, but David didn't get the message, so that when he showed up to say goodbye, only Carolyn was left at the house. It was eerie talking to her now; she sounded uncannily like her older sister. They both had a way of swallowing the last word of a sentence, a habit that, intentional or not, meant that you had to listen carefully to the very end.

"Are you free some night to get out for a drink?" he asked. "I know I could use a change of scenery."

They agreed on the time—nine o'clock the next night—but not the place, as neither of them knew the area well enough to suggest one. David promised to scout out Birmingham, then call her back with a suitable location.

.   .   .

THE NEXT DAY he sat in the passenger seat, his father driving thirty-five down Woodward. David wanted to say something, but his father was keeping the car in the lane and everyone else was passing them easily enough.

"I want you to call my lawyer," his father said.

"Steve Bergen? Why?"

"His son, Peter. He's about your age, I'd guess."

"What's it about?" David asked.

"A job," Sol said.

"You're going back to work?"

"No, they need someone like you."

"You know, Dad, I'm already a partner in a law firm. I mean, I appreciate the suggestion, but . . ." Just like the old man, he thought, always nudging, a true marine, never happy just to hold the ground he had.

"But what?"

"Move back to Detroit? For good? What about my job? My life in Denver?"

"You should move back."

"Why would anyone move here?"

"It's your home, for one thing. Your family is here."

"You and Mom."

"What," his father said, "we don't count? And the other thing, just as important? You need to get out of Denver."

David sat in silence. Every once in a while his father said something that made sense, like a savant who could cut through to the simple truth: he needed to leave Denver. Till now he hadn't thought of Detroit.

*   *   *

THAT NIGHT DAVID waited for Carolyn at the bar. The bartender, young, hair spiked, came over with a What'll-it-be look. Here David was, forty-five, and he still hadn't settled on a usual drink. He ordered a gin and tonic, the first thing that came into his mind.

He had chosen this bar by walking the streets of Birmingham. His mistake was not to look for a TV. This bar didn't have one, and so now he was sitting alone, with nothing to do and nowhere to look except at the mirror behind the infantry lines of liquor bottles.

His mother, he'd learned that afternoon, had moved up to first on the waiting list at the nursing home. His father had entrusted him (enlisted him, really) to take her out there next week, to show her around. It was hard to know how she'd take this. He expected the worst, but so far she seemed resigned to the idea, or perhaps unable to comprehend it.

"Another?" asked the bartender.

"Sure," David replied, trying to approximate a drinker. He had a brief memory of Cory, a waking nightmare that flared up now and again. He shook his head to rid himself of the feeling; it always took some kind of physical effort.

He turned to survey the bar, expecting to find Carolyn, now fifteen minutes late. Natalie was always punctual, but he'd known her when she was young and perhaps didn't know better. And then Carolyn surprised him.

"Haven't been here in years," she said as she slid onto the stool next to him.

"Carolyn." He wouldn't have recognized her. She was still blond, but her hair was shorter and she'd filled out into a woman, more attractive than the spindly teenager she'd been. She wore designer jeans and a white blouse. After an awkward pause, they accomplished a lopsided hug, both of them teetering on the edge of their bar stools.

"Getcha something?" the bartender asked. "He's two up on you."

She studied David's gin and tonic. "Bushmills, straight up," she said.

David looked at his drink in a new, feminine light. Still, he didn't like whiskey enough. Perhaps vodka. Or just red wine. Red wine was acceptable.

He noticed her hands on the bar, the same long fingers he remembered Natalie having, except Carolyn wore a wedding ring, the yellow diamond almost bursting from the band.

"You're married," he said.

"Aren't you?"

"I was once. Not now."

"I'm sorry," she said.

"Don't be," he told her. "I'm beginning to see the advantage of being single."

"Which is?"

"Only one person to make happy."

Her drink arrived and she raised it for a toast. Their glasses clinked. "So, how's it going?" she asked.

"With what?"

"Keeping that one person happy."

Well enough, he allowed, and then changed the subject. He was pretty sure women liked him because he listened. It came to him naturally, and he'd honed it from years of estate planning, when he would sit and listen to people say what they wanted till they got tired of listening to themselves lie. Then he'd draw up a plan that pleased the person paying the bill.

Her husband was a lawyer, intellectual property. Carolyn herself worked in advertising. At home they had daily help, a woman from El Salvador. Carolyn's son went to private school. These were the details from L.A. "You can play tennis outside in January," she said.

"Do you?"

"I did, once."

"Tell me about your son," he said.

He studied her while she talked, the angular face, the golden hair, the perfect white line of her teeth. He felt something. He didn't want to, but he did. The implications of this were so uniformly unsettling that he ordered another drink, this time a glass of cabernet, which seemed manly enough, despite its French name.

Carolyn said, "It's a little weird, being here with you."

"How so?"

" 'Cause I think I had a crush on you when I was . . . well, a little girl. I was jealous of my sister because she had you."

"I'm flattered," he said.

"It was about Natalie. I was always jealous of her. She was older, more beautiful. But it wasn't a bad jealousy. I looked up to her."

"She wasn't more beautiful."

She looked down. "You're sweet," she said. He thought perhaps that she blushed. Her modesty touched him. Maybe her beauty was something her husband no longer commented on. It was possible, he knew, to disappear in a marriage.

"You must miss Natalie," he said.

She nodded, and looked down. "Terribly," she said. "There was so much—" She stopped talking.

"What?"

"So much left for us to do," she said. "And Dirk, too. Really, I barely knew him."

"Didn't he ever live with you?"

Dirk, she said, had lived with his father. This was agreed

upon by his parents, the obvious choice to them when they split up, because Dirk was black. Dirk's father, though, was indifferent at best, and Dirk was really raised by his father's oldest friend, adopted every way but legally. The FBI was Dirk's idea. "He wanted to set the world right, get everyone in line," said Carolyn. "That's what Natalie always said."

"What were Natalie and Dirk doing the night they were killed?"

"No one knows. They spent a lot of time together after her marriage ended. Dirk's daughter was out of college. Shelly, his wife, likes her space. Nat and Dirk kept each other company. My mother liked it that they had a friendship. She felt things with her family were finally coming together. Except I wasn't there."

David nodded. He felt a longing, a terrible ache for his son, so he smiled.

"Do you have kids?" she asked.

"No," he said. "But I can imagine."

IV

CAROLYN LIKED HIM, had always liked him. She'd realized this as a girl and saw it again now: there was no artifice with David Halpert, no tics or anger or phobias or recklessness hidden in some shadow of his personality. Not that he didn't have some of these things, but the lights were on. Also, he was not a bad-looking guy. He was losing his hair and he'd put on some weight since high school—who hadn't?—but he still could look at her directly and get her attention. A man who could look you in the eye was not to be taken lightly.

She remembered her sister's devotion to David. Carolyn wanted to feel so strongly about a man that nothing else mattered, but it hadn't gone that way. Marty had come along at the right time. In the end, she'd pursued him and he'd surrendered. She saw in him a steady man, a good provider, someone who didn't mind being left alone. A man, in short, not unlike her father. She felt secure with Marty. She never really had to worry about anything.

She asked why David had become a lawyer.

"Lack of imagination," he said.

"What else would you have been?"

"I'm still trying to figure it out."

He didn't elaborate, and soon she found herself talking about her mother. The subject was too depressing, so she excused herself to go to the ladies' room, where she could check her face. David stood when she got up from the table, as her father would have; as Marty once did, but no longer.

•   •   •

DAVID STOOD AGAIN when she returned to the table.

"Tell me what went wrong with your marriage. And then what went right."

"Well, we fell in love. It wasn't all bad, at the beginning. Then we fell out of love. What about you? Why did you get married?"

"I thought Marty would make a good husband, and it seemed like the right time."

"I see," he said.

She had in effect told him that she wasn't in love with her husband, and he had understood immediately.

"I was young," she said.

"Then there's the boy. That makes it complicated, right? No kids and you're like me, you both walk away and it's no harm, no foul."

"I'm sure," she said, meaning the opposite.

He shrugged. "Well, you should be happy."

"How can you say that? You don't know me."

"It's just how I want to think of you," he said.

It was like therapy, talking to David; actually, he was better than her therapist in Beverly Hills. David was a much quicker study, and refreshingly direct. There was a sadness to him, but he didn't try to hide it—or couldn't—and that made him that much more attractive. She could think of a dozen women back in L.A. who would crawl over each other to have dinner with this man.

"So tell me, David," she said, "why isn't there a woman in your life?"

"How do you know there's not?"

"I don't think there is."

"You're right," he admitted.

. . .

HE POURED WINE into a tumbler. They were in his living room, walls the color of pudding, an Ansel Adams photo (nice enough, but out of place), carpet the color of dirt, a greenish couch she was sitting on. Before she got married, if a man had brought her to a dump like this she wouldn't have considered him a serious contender. Tonight they'd gone to a liquor store for wine, then walked back here like a couple of teenagers. She realized that once she stopped asking him questions he became talkative, funny. She was conscious of what she was doing, that she was a married woman in the apartment of an unmarried man, the ex-boyfriend of her dead sister.

"Here's to you," he said. He clinked his glass to hers. "I must tell you, I think I'm drunk. I don't drink often, but . . ."

"And yet you keep drinking," she said. She was feeling a bit tipsy herself.

She had cheated on Marty twice before; she had considered doing it far more than that. Offers were surprisingly abundant. Just last week she had gone to lunch with the guy from her firm who was to head up the marketing campaign for a new movie. They'd been seated about five seconds when he looked at her ring and said, "So, are you *happily* married?"

She was appalled by his rudeness, by his lack of respect for her as a professional, and most of all by the world and its excessive store of desperation.

She wasn't feeling any of that now. She just wanted to be reckless.

"Set down your glass," she said. He did as he was told. She moved to him and kissed him. He was surprised at first, but he quickly adjusted. It was thrilling, almost like being young again. She hadn't felt anything like it in years.

V

DAVID PACED IN his kitchen, wanting to call Carolyn. In the last six days they'd had dinner three times. She wouldn't sleep with him. He'd asked—it seemed almost insulting not to—but only once, at the second dinner. She was married, after all. The last time he called she told him not to call again, but he had a hard time believing her. Yes, she was married, but she was available. He could feel it. He decided to call anyway. Maybe she would pick up. In fact, she did.

"Come over," he said.

She hung up without a word. Half an hour later, she surprised him at his door. He greeted her, but she entered without speaking, set her purse on the dining table, threw her coat over a chair, slipped out of her shoes. She walked to the bedroom. David gave himself a moment to watch the elaborate design on the back pockets of her jeans swing back and forth.

He took a deep breath, conscious of it, and then walked into the bedroom. He found her studying the bed, arms crossed, head bowed, a picture of agony.

"I can't," she said.

"Then don't."

"But I want to."

"Then do."

. . .

LATER, HE HELD her in his arms, drifting in and out of sleep.

"What are we doing?" she said.

It was a good question. It was new and exciting. He liked her, and he liked himself when he was with her. He hadn't thought about it beyond that. He stayed quiet till she gave him a nudge, a pointy elbow to his ribcage.

"I just like you," he said.

"That's your answer?"

"I don't have an answer. What do you think we're doing?"

"I'm a sucker for attention," she said.

He was hoping for higher standards, but he'd take it.

"And you were Natalie's boyfriend," she said. "I always wanted what she had, and suddenly I have it."

"It isn't personal, you're saying."

"It's very personal. But I'm married. I have a child. I have to go back home."

"I'm thinking of moving back here," he said.

The words were out, and he found that they were settling

well. The idea of a move, of change, lifted his mood. He was ready to start something new.

"Moving back?"

"It's home, where I'm from. It seems like a silly, hopeless thing to do, so maybe it will work for me."

"It's like moving back to Hiroshima," she said.

"People live there now, I'm pretty sure." In the darkness he thought he saw her smile, or grimace. It didn't matter which. He had made a decision.

1994

I

Marlon heard it, his name, three times, like an echo. He handed the joint back to Eric. "Gonna have to go."

"What for?"

"My dad's calling."

"I ain't heard nothing."

"I hear him," Marlon said. In truth, he didn't want to go. He had a good buzz and he just wanted to hang here, behind his friend's house, and let the afternoon wash over him, time sliding by like a river. It was what made this summer special, the afternoon high, enjoying what adults got to enjoy.

Marlon spent most every day with Eric. Sometimes they said they were brothers, and they meant it like blood. Better than blood. Eric was someone he could count on. Eric lived with his mother and a real older brother, and neither one was ever around, except the brother in the middle of the night. His mother could be gone for days, and sometimes there was nothing to eat. Eric took to hiding food in his room, so his brother wouldn't get it.

"You lucky, man," Eric said.

" 'Cause I gotta go?" Marlon asked.

" 'Cause you got an old man who wants you to."

"Usually he's pissed at me," Marlon said, and this was true. Marlon could hardly do anything right. "He's always on me at home," Marlon continued. "About doing good in school, what am I gonna do with my life, all that shit."

Eric took a long drag, then talked while holding in the smoke. "So, that's gotta really suck, huh? Being loved too much?"

. . .

HE WALKED IN the back door and there was his father, Everett, waiting for him, showered and scrubbed. His father always did a lot of scrubbing to get the steel plant off of him. They had chemicals at the plant that floated in the air and left everything stiff and sticky, as if it had been coated in hairspray. Just last weekend Marlon had watched his mother dump the laundry on the floor and out came his father's work clothes, frozen in the circular shape of the laundry hamper.

"How you feeling, son?" his father asked.

"Good."

"Took you a while to get here."

"Just came on my own. Didn't hear nothing."

"Anything," his mother said. She was at the stove, and always on him to talk white.

His father tilted his head, a way of giving an order. Marlon took his place at the table. It wasn't so bad to sit here with a nice buzz. Also, he was starving. When the food hit the table, he dug in. At one point he looked up and both of his parents were staring at him.

"You want to take a breath?" his father asked.

"Hungry," he explained. He finished his chicken, took the plate to the sink, and then headed for the back door. His parents were talking about some neighbor. He figured he'd head back to Eric's while it was still light, maybe watch a video or something.

"Marlon Booker!" his mother yelled.

"Sorry, Mom." He was supposed to ask to be excused. He put on his best hangdog look and slunk back to the table. "May I?" he asked. "Please."

"Yes," she said.

"No," said his father.

"But . . ." His father never said no.

"I want to talk to you. After you help your mother clean up the kitchen."

"What the—"

"Watch your mouth," his mother said.

He stopped talking. He wasn't going to win with these two. Better to stay quiet and try to save the buzz.

•   •   •

"You're stoned," his father said. They were in Marlon's room, the place he went to be alone. Marlon hated it when his father came in like he owned the place.

"What?" Marlon said, stalling.

"You heard me. Thirteen years old, Marlon, and you're showing up to dinner stoned out of your mind. You think that's cool? Where'd you get it, that McCall kid?"

"Dad, there's so much smoke on the street, it's like we in Mexico."

"*We're* in Mexico," his father corrected.

"Shit."

"Marlon!"

"What are we talking 'bout here? English grades or drugs?"

"Drugs."

"Well, it's not like it's crack. Weed never hurt no one."

"Smoking," the old man said, "hurts everyone."

Marlon just waited, and longed for this talk to be over.

"What do you want to make of yourself?" his father asked. Always that question: a week didn't go by without that question getting asked. It was as if his father couldn't stand the suspense of not knowing what his son would do for work twenty years from now.

"Don't want to work in no steel plant," Marlon said. This was true. No way, no how did he want to go to that horrible place, hot and loud with machinery that sounded like metal breaking. Not that he had any idea where he did want to go. His friends all thought they'd make it at b-ball or rap, which Marlon thought was just stupid. The world already had too many stars, and not enough people doing useful things.

"Smartest thing you've said all night," his father said.

Marlon waited for him to say more, but nothing came. "We done?" Marlon asked.

"You're grounded," Everett said. "You're not to leave the property without a parent. One month. At night, no TV. You stay here in your room."

"Dad!" He made fists, squeezed them so tight he could feel his nails digging into his skin. It was the only way to keep from shouting.

"This is serious," his father said.

"Weed, Dad? You can't stop that."

"I can try."

"You gonna lose."

His father left on that. Marlon flopped back on his bed, but the buzz was gone.

II

Everett didn't know if he would beat this cancer thing— the doctor said there was a decent chance—but what kept him awake at night was Marlon. He knew a man couldn't control the cancer cells in his body, and perhaps the same could be said of his son. Still, he reasoned it had to be otherwise; God, he thought, wouldn't have given us sons if we couldn't have an impact. He wouldn't have sent one to us himself. Everett just needed a little time. It was important. There was some shit in the world now; it was easier to go astray, and more dangerous when you did. If he could just get another five or six years he could see the kid off right.

He climbed into his truck, a '68 GMC pickup with three on the tree, touchy as hell when you wanted to find reverse and half junkyard under the hood. The odometer was broken, which was fine with Everett, because he didn't really want to know. The truck's upper reaches were still army green, which faded as the steel got closer to the road till there was nothing but rust from the salt of a quarter century of Michigan winters. The effect was something like a turning oak leaf. There was a spot on the floorboard where Everett used to be able to see the road pass beneath him, which he liked, but he'd had to close it with duct tape so he didn't get splashed when it rained. What Everett liked about the truck: nothing bad could happen to him in it. It wasn't anything to protect.

Everett needed his friend Dirk now, and he really didn't have much of a favor to call in. He just needed him. Over thirty years they'd known each other, and in all that time Dirk had asked Everett for only one thing. They were about twelve, walking toward school, through light flurries, stepping over a curb stacked with coffee-colored slush. "Don't tell no one," Dirk said, "that I have a white mother."

"I won't," Everett said. And he never had.

• • •

EVERETT WANTED TO wait before starting the chemo, but the doctor wasn't having it. There wasn't a day to lose, said this scrawny, curly-haired guy, the kind of white kid who probably got beat up on the playground. Almost three weeks had been frittered away and now it was time to act, said the doctor.

"Where'd you go to medical school at?" Everett asked, fishing for a different diagnosis.

"McGill."

That set Everett back. He'd never heard of the place, but the doctor said it with such pride that Everett figured he should know it, at least if he was going to keep pretending he was the kind of man who might actually know about medical schools. "That's in—"

"Montreal."

"Ah, well, they teach you up in Canada that sometimes a man's got to be ready?"

The doctor set his clipboard down on the corner of the sink and sat on the stool, so that he was lower than Everett, who was sitting on the bed in his T-shirt and underwear. There ought to be a law, Everett thought, where you didn't have to talk to a doctor unless you were dressed.

"Look, Mr. Booker, I wouldn't expect you to be ready. No one is ready for cancer. But the fact is, cancer cells don't wait. They eat the body alive. We kill them now or they kill you later. And only a little later."

"You said before they might anyway."

"It's my job to try to stop them. Don't you want to?"

Of course he did. He just didn't want to tell his wife. Patrice would go all loopy on him and want him to quit his job, and then what was he going to do all day?

"You sure I'm going to have to stop working?" He hadn't told the doctor that Bethlehem was closing the plant anyway.

The doctor nodded. "Yes. You work in a steel plant, right? You're going to be weak at first, and not feeling well. There's no alternative, really."

"A man's got to work to be a man."

"We'll get you back as soon as we can."

"Why'd you come to the States?" Everett asked.

"My wife grew up here."

"In Detroit?"

"Yes."

"A white girl?"

"Yes, from Southfield, actually. Not a girl. She's thirty-three now."

"Still young."

"Yes," the doctor admitted.

"You think I coulda caught this cancer working in the steel plant?"

The doctor opened up his hands, soft and pink, hands like you found in a library. "Who knows? Maybe. Then again, you said you used to smoke. That's the surefire way to get lung cancer."

"I got a boy," Everett said. "He's gonna need me."

"Then we better get going," said the doctor. He looked down, and then up again. "But, Mr. Booker," he said, "I can make you no guarantees. Now is the time to put your affairs in order. Write up a will, if you don't have one. Make sure your wife knows where your important papers are. And if there's any unfinished business with anyone who matters to you, now is the time to finish it."

"You're saying I'm going to die."

"I'm saying I don't know when," he said. "I say this to all my patients. Take my advice. There's nothing to lose in this. With a little luck, you'll be organized and alive."

III

Dirk's arches ached, standing around all day in shit-kicker boots popular with a certain type of brother in a certain type of business. Miles had even commented on them, and Dirk told him about a store on Grand River Avenue that would have his size, fourteen, which wasn't exactly Bob Lanier but it was big. Miles had ambition in heroin. He sensed a comeback. He'd apparently trained with remnants of YBI, and this meant he was likely to be a disciplined trafficker. He'd caught Dirk's attention because he was quiet, operated with a very small crew, and was said to move size, God knew how. Dirk promised Miles quantities equal to Miles's ambition; the goods would come over in trucks filled with auto parts made at a Delphi plant in Ontario. The story was Dirk's idea. Everyone, he told his boss, McMahon, believed that the auto industry had privilege at border crossings. Today he'd driven across the Ambassador Bridge and had Miles meet McMahon in Windsor. McMahon was hopeless for normal under-cover work, but he was white bread enough, and nervous enough, to play a crooked Canadian with auto industry connections.

"Where'd you get a name like Miles?" Dirk asked while they waited in line at Canadian customs. Dirk was fishing; you never knew what would come out.

Miles looked over. "What's it to you?"

"Just wondered."

"Where'd you get a name like Barry?"

From the FBI, Dirk thought. "My momma, after her pops," he said.

Miles looked straight ahead. "I got mine from my momma, too."

"You're the first brother I've ever met with that name," Dirk said.

"That's 'cause my momma's white."

"Wow. That's something," Dirk said.

"She's a good woman, my mom. She'd have a heart attack, seeing me here with you."

"Yeah," Dirk said. "Mine would, too."

"What you tell yours, when she asks you what you're doing all the time?"

"She's dead."

"You're a lucky man," Miles said.

. . .

Dirk loved being home. He loved the house, with its solid walls and wood floors, its open spaces. After a day on the streets, coming home was like getting back to the garden. He could hear his wife, Shelly, in the kitchen with their daughter. They were talking, conspiring maybe. He couldn't make it out, but he liked listening to them. Not much of a talker himself, Dirk liked the voices of women.

"Whatcha doing, Daddy?" Michelle called out, walking toward him now from the kitchen. It was shocking to look up sometimes and see how tall she'd become.

"Resting," he answered.

"Long day."

"Very," he agreed.

"Mom wants to know if you want a drink."

A minute later his daughter served him a vodka and soda, the perfect antidote to a day fighting drugs. He asked her about her schoolwork, if she wanted his help with her math. He would have helped, but he was thankful when she said no. He didn't want to move.

The phone rang. Shelly got it in the kitchen. He watched as Michelle stood perfectly still, listening.

"One of your pals?" he asked.

"Naw, Mom wouldn't be talking to them for so long."

.   .   .

AFTER DINNER MICHELLE went upstairs to call her friends—
Dirk allowed her a phone jack in her room, but not a separate line—and Dirk and Shelly cleaned up the kitchen.
He cleared, then dried. She didn't trust him to wash her
good dishes any more than she trusted the dishwashing
machine he'd bought her when the last COLA raise came
through. This was fine. He liked drying, found it soothing,
as he did many domestic chores.

"Everett's coming over," she said, hands in the soap.

"Great. What night?"

"Tonight. Says he needs to talk to you."

"What about?"

"He wouldn't tell me, and believe me, I asked at least
five times."

"What time's he coming?"

"Ten."

"Jesus, I'll be asleep by then."

"Not tonight, baby."

"You could have checked with me," Dirk said.

"You'd never say no to Everett." She handed him the
last dish and let the drain suck the water from the sink.

"Will you wait up for me?" he asked.

"I'd like to, but I don't know."

"Can I wake you?"

She smiled at him. "You'd better make it worth my
while."

• • •

HE FIXED HIMSELF a second vodka soda, careful with the proportions; he even sliced a small wedge of lime, then made a perpendicular cut and ran the meat of the lime around the edge of his glass. A second drink was a rare occurrence, usually saved for the cold-weather holidays, watching the Lions lose on Thanksgiving, or champagne on New Year's, for him always the longest night of the year. Tomorrow wouldn't start till noon, when he had to drive out to Novi to meet Miles, and he was backup tomorrow night on a stakeout, now that Collins's wife was in labor. Dirk hated surveillance. The time-suck (as Michelle would say) nature of it, the utter boredom of watching criminals in their natural habitats.

Dirk heard Everett's pickup park at the curb, and so he had the front door open as Everett walked up. Everett had become a stocky man; tonight he wore the Wayne State T-shirt that Dirk had given him. Everett seemed prouder of Dirk's degree than Dirk did himself.

"Hey, man," Everett said. Dirk responded with a hey, a handshake that was close, almost a chest bump, the way the football players did it nowadays. "Thanks," Everett said, and they both understood for what: for seeing Everett on a Tuesday night, late, when they both ought to have been in bed.

"Marlon came home high yesterday," Everett said once Dirk got him a Strohs and seated him in the living room.

Dirk nodded. No big surprise. Marlon, he suspected,

would always be a worry, but he liked the kid, too, liked his spirit, the basic rebellion in him, whether it was sneaking out of the house when he was still in diapers or Crazy Gluing the mailbox shut on the day he expected his grades to show up.

"Michelle ever?" Everett asked, leaving off the words "smoke pot."

"Not that I know of, but I might not always know. What did you do about Marlon?"

"I grounded him for a month, mostly 'cause I don't know what else to do. He hates me."

"What did he say?"

"He said he wasn't smoking rocks, so I should relax."

"The first part's good news."

"He said you can't stop weed."

"Might be true," said Dirk.

"So I'm just supposed to let him be a pothead?"

"No," Dirk said. He understood the frustration. His cell phone rang, the one the criminals called. Dirk looked at the number. It was Miles.

"It's my job calling," he explained to Everett.

Miles wanted Dirk to come to a party, then protested when Dirk declined. "It's not personal," Dirk said.

"And why we got to meet in Novi?" Miles asked. "Had to find it on a map. Nothing but white people out there."

"So you should feel at home, on account of your mom."

"You leave her out of this."

"So don't bring her," Dirk said. Today he'd received the

FBI file on Miles. Miles was his real name. He'd graduated from high school at Liggett School. He'd gotten a 3.5 his first two years in Ann Arbor, which meant he definitely knew where Novi was. With mandatory sentencing, he was going away for a while. It was going to be a pity.

More silence from Miles. Dirk could feel him calculating.

"You don't trust me, don't show up," Dirk said. He hung up and smiled at Everett. "Sorry."

"And I got cancer," Everett said.

. . .

MILES DIDN'T SHOW. Dirk couldn't believe it. He'd never lost someone so quickly.

He called downtown and then headed for Everett's, figuring he'd have that talk with Marlon now that he had three and a half hours till the stakeout. The talk was the first thing he'd promised Everett the night before. The second was that if Everett didn't make it, Dirk would check in on Patrice, his wife. "That pension ain't much, and she would only get half," Everett said. The third request was Marlon. "He's gonna need a father. If I ain't around, that's got to be you. I don't know how else to say it."

There was obvious symmetry to the request, but this occurred to Dirk only later. At this moment, he simply felt that it was right. He would have done anything for Everett, and welcomed the chance to do it. All the relationships he had with his blood relatives—his biological mother, his half-sisters—were hopelessly complicated, burdened with decisions made before he could reason, some before he was born. What he had with Everett was different.

"Whatever he needs," Dirk promised. "It comes to that, it will be as if he's my own."

. . .

DIRK DROVE EVERETT'S street at a prowl, the black-tinted windows of his car lowered so Marlon could see him if Marlon happened to be on the street. These streets were working-class black, except for the odd Eastern European holdout who hadn't fled with the rest of the white people twenty-five years ago. The whites here were Ukrainian, Polish, Belorussian, and Dirk found it odd that he even knew this. Come from Africa and you're black. Come from Europe and they got it separated out by neighborhood.

Marlon was standing in the front yard when Dirk pulled in. There was another boy with him, and two others materialized by the time Dirk climbed out of the car.

"Hey, Marlon," Dirk said. He was a skinny kid, which he must have gotten from Patrice's family.

"Hey, Uncle Dirk."

"Can we look inside?" asked one of the kids, peering in the car. The kid was wearing a T-shirt with a picture of a white guy in mirrored shades pressing a .44 to a puppy's head. Under the photo was a tag line that read, "Say Nice Things About Detroit."

"What's with the shirt?" Dirk asked.

"What you mean?"

"I don't get it."

"Like, say nice things about Detroit," the kid said, "or the white dude shoots the dog."

Dirk had to admit it was funny. He opened the passenger door and Marlon's three friends stuck their heads inside the car. "A Blaupunkt," said one. "Real leather," said another, running his finger across the seat. Marlon hung back.

"What you pay for this?" asked one of the kids.

"It was free."

"Free? No way."

"Sure, got it from a drug dealer."

They all looked at him. Probably they thought he was a drug dealer.

"Sure. You use a car in the commission of a crime, you forfeit the car. This baby now belongs to the U.S. government."

"Why you got it?" asked the skinny one.

"I work for the government."

"Yeah, you do," said the chubby kid.

Dirk showed him the badge. "FBI." At that the third kid took off running. The others just watched him go without amusement or surprise, as if this were something he did often. In the silence Dirk could feel the heat in the driveway. To Marlon he said, "Let's you and me go for a ride."

"I'm grounded. Can't leave."

Dirk went inside to find Patrice. He found her at the kitchen table, facing toward the back of the house, sitting, he realized, in front of two fans. "Hello, Dirk," she said in that way she had, which, oddly enough, reminded him of his mother.

"How you been, Patrice?"

"Oh, you know. Everett says you're going to talk some sense into Marlon."

"Nothing Everett probably hasn't said already. Sometimes it helps to hear it from another corner."

"How's that Michelle?"

"She's good. Growing up, you know. Hardly recognize her sometimes when I come home."

"You're a lucky man, Dirk."

"That's true."

"After you get done with Marlon, maybe you could talk to Everett, too."

"What for?" Dirk asked.

"Because I know he's sick, and I can't very well help him if he won't admit it."

IV

THEY DROVE SOUTH. Marlon started to put his sneakers on the dash, the way he could in the pickup, and then thought better of it. This interior was sweet. Half a dozen cows must have died just to come up with all the leather. The thing was, it wasn't really Dirk's car. It was more of a loaner from the FBI. Renting a house was one thing, but a car was different. Marlon thought a man should really own his car, even if it wasn't nice like this one. That way, he could always control where he was going.

They were driving on Gratiot, headed down to the Ren Cen. Marlon could see the towers, a white-gray, like the sky.

"Let's ride the People Mover," Dirk said.

"Why?" Marlon asked.

"Coleman Young built the thing, so somebody's got to ride it. It's your civic duty."

They climbed the stairs and Dirk paid the fare. When the car moved, Marlon turned to the glass. There was something like a view from the train car, elevated above the street. He looked back to the river and Windsor, forward to Greektown, Tiger Stadium to the west, and the east side, where lots were going back to pasture and you could hear crickets on summer nights.

"Nice view, huh?"

"Man, you can see the whole world up here," Marlon said.

"That's why we're here," Dirk said. "I'm trying to lift your vision."

He took Marlon to Greektown. It wasn't really Detroit, it was like a theater for white people, but Marlon knew Dirk liked it because it was clean. White and black mixed on Monroe Street. Dirk stopped at a bakery.

"It's baklava. Try it. It's made with honey."

Marlon took a bite. It was sweet and light and sticky. Also good. "This is all right," he said.

"What's this I hear, you're smoking dope?" Dirk said.

Marlon should have known this was coming. His father had put Dirk up to it. "It ain't nothing," Marlon said. True enough. The true idiots did other things. From what Marlon could see, getting high harmed no one.

"It's something, all right," Dirk said. "You ever meet a pothead who did anything with his life?"

"It's the crackheads that's fucked up."

"Watch your tongue with me," Dirk said. "I'm not here for my health. I'm here for you. You're thirteen, you've got all sorts of choices to make. But the choices you make now can stay with you your whole life."

"Gotta decide now to be Mr. FBI?"

"Right now I'd like you to decide not to do drugs. We'll build from there."

"I know why my father sent you," Marlon said.

"Why?"

" 'Cause, like, what's he gonna say? Be like me, work in a smelly steel plant they gonna close anyhow? Don't get no education, drop outta high school?"

"Your father has a high school diploma."

"GED," Marlon said. Even the old man didn't stick it out in high school. Dirk, of course, had a college degree, which meant that at this moment Marlon had to stand there and listen to him.

"You know," Dirk said, "you do drugs, and I can bust you. And I will."

"Hey, you the one with the big black Mercedes with the Blow Punk stereo and the subwoofer under the back seat. You just like playing Mr. Drug Dealer, if you ask me."

"I didn't," Dirk said.

"You did."

"I didn't ask you, Marlon."

"I'm just saying."

Marlon could see he'd hit a chord. Not easy to do with Dirk. The man never got riled. He was cold and calculating, something he probably got from his white mother.

"I risk my life," Dirk said, "to clean up the streets. *I'm* just saying I'd appreciate it if you did your little part."

"These streets ain't never gonna be clean," Marlon told him. "I'd rather have the car."

2006

I

They drove to Palmer Woods, her mother silent in the passenger seat, staring blankly out the window. They were in the city limits now, but it was quite nice, streets lined with trees just starting to turn. Dirk had bought a house here on FBI pay. Now Shelly lived in it alone. Michelle was a journalist at a small paper in Texas. Why Texas Carolyn didn't know, but she could guess: Texas was far away.

Shelly had invited them. She wanted to give Tina a photo album, dozens of pictures, all of them now digitally copied, printed, and placed in a leather-bound album. What a family, Carolyn thought, where a mother doesn't have pictures of her son. Certainly there were no framed photos in the townhouse, and Carolyn didn't remember any from their home. Dirk's was a life hidden from sight.

Carolyn asked her mother why she hadn't raised her son.

"The world today is different than it was then. I did what I thought was best for him."

"By giving him away?"

Her mother turned from the window, looked at her. "You know nothing," she said.

"I'm just asking, Mom. You sent your son to live with someone else. Why?"

"I am through talking about it."

•   •   •

THE HOUSE WAS brick, elegantly laid out, with a turret at each end and a Tudor-style roof. The front door was wood and enormous. When Shelly swung it open she seemed small, though in fact she was just shy of six feet tall.

"Oh, I'm so glad you came," Shelly said, as if she half expected that they wouldn't. She led them to the living room, lined with bookcases, each book without its dust jacket. Shelly offered drinks.

"A vodka tonic," Tina said.

It was two in the afternoon. *What the hell,* Carolyn thought.

"Make it two."

Carolyn sat on the couch with her mother. They looked at the album, lying there on the table. Her mother made no move for the book. Carolyn was curious; her mother, she guessed, was fearful. Carolyn tried to imagine what it might be like to live here, among the long shadows and all those books without covers. It held a certain appeal. Sometimes in California she felt depressed by all the light.

"Are you okay?" she asked her mother. Lately she asked this often. Carolyn felt the loss of Natalie deeply, as if some vital part of her were missing. She knew she would never be the same, but Natalie was her sister and not her child, and nothing she felt could compare to what her mother was going through.

Shelly returned with the drinks, carried on a silver platter, a white wine for herself.

"Please," she said, pushing the album at them. "Take a look."

Shelly had, curiously, organized the photos backward, with the older Dirk first. Tina slowly turned the pages. There were a half-dozen pictures of Dirk with Natalie and Carolyn (few of which Carolyn remembered), several pages of Dirk as a boy with his surrogate family, one or two with a man who must have been the one who fathered him, and, at the end, a very young Dirk, perhaps six months old, held by his mother. Carolyn had never seen a photo of her mother from that time. Tina looked a lot like Natalie.

"Wow, Mom," Carolyn said. "Look at you!"

Her mother was crying. She wiped at her eyes with the back of her hand. What it must have been like then—young and beautiful in a new country with a black baby.

"They're great, aren't they?" Shelly said.

"Where did you get that last one?" Tina asked.

"Dirk had it. He kept it hidden in a book. It was very important to him."

"Oh God," Tina said. "I didn't know what to do."

"About what?" Carolyn asked.

"About Dirk. How to raise him. It was a different time."

"You did marry a black man," Shelly said.

"I knew it was a little unusual, but I didn't think it would be such a big deal here in Detroit. In America."

"But it was a big deal," Shelly said.

"Oh my, yes. It was as if I'd broken the law, which I had, really. It wasn't allowed in Michigan then. So we got married in Ohio."

"That was a pretty good hint," Shelly said.

"Yes, but I ignored it. We were young, and in love."

Carolyn found that she'd finished her vodka. She would have liked another.

"Joseph," she said. She turned to Carolyn. "That was Dirk's father's name. We were strangers to each other. When it became clear we weren't going to spend our lives together, I think we both felt it would be better if Dirk grew up in a Negro household. That's what you called it back then. Even the words were different."

"Didn't you miss him?" asked Shelly.

"I visited," Tina said. "I wrote him letters. You have to understand, I believed it was what was best for him. A black child growing up with whites? It just didn't happen. But I took him on excursions. He loved the Henry Ford Museum, so I took him, probably once a month until he was a teenager. He loved it there, the old cars kept just so.

When he got older and he was living with the Bookers, he really just wanted to be with his friends. It seemed easier for everyone to let things be."

Shelly seemed to know this story. Carolyn remembered when she first learned of Dirk. She was at the dinner table when her mother told her she had a brother. "I was married once before I knew your father. My first husband and I had a son, your half-brother. He'd like to meet you."

He'd like to meet you. It was a clever way to put it. A half hour later Dirk pulled up in one of those big black cars he drove. He got out, six-three, a big 'fro, long, long legs covered in jeans, a brown T-shirt covering half of his biceps. He was black. Carolyn's breath caught. Natalie laughed. She was about fifteen then.

"Your first husband was black, Mom?" Natalie asked right then. She immediately loved Dirk. Carolyn envied how open Natalie could be to everything; it was one more thing she missed about her sister. Carolyn was always more reserved. At first she had felt almost offended by the existence of Dirk. Secrets—important secrets—had been kept from her.

Carolyn noticed that during Dirk's first visit her mother stood back, almost out of the way, as if she were merely an observer of the events. Carolyn came to understand that her mother was embarrassed by her history but proud of Dirk. Natalie said that he'd been in line to run the Detroit office of the FBI, but that he'd retired instead. Their father, it turned out, had left him money.

• • •

THE SECOND DRINK never came. It wasn't to be that kind of visit. They stood.

"The Bookers weren't at the funeral," Tina said.

"Sylvia and Tom are dead. Patrice has disappeared, and Everett, as I'm sure you know, died. His son, Marlon, is still around. He stays here every once in a blue moon."

That seemed to settle things. Soon they were out the door. For the first time in hours Carolyn thought of David, what he might be doing, and then of Marty. She wondered if her problem was simply that she'd had it too easy, what with parents who kept her and raised her in comfort, with white skin and blond hair. Dirk had had none of that, and yet looking at those pictures, she thought he looked happy enough. Of course, if a picture was worth a thousand words, it was also true that often none of those words were true.

Her mother sat next to her, seatbelt across her overcoat, hands clasped over the photo album in her lap. They were on the expressway now, driving fast by the gray walls.

"Do you regret it, Mom?"

"Regret what, exactly?"

"Leaving Dirk's father. Giving up Dirk."

She exhaled.

"I guess that's a yes," Carolyn said.

"It's years too late for that now," Tina said.

II

DAVID WALKED BEHIND his parents, pulling his mother's suitcase, his gait intentionally slow so as not to run them over. He wondered what genius had put wheels on suitcases, and why, say, Ford or GM hadn't thought of it first.

His mother leaned against his father and he against her, so that their shoulders touched, leaving a teepee of light between them. Finally they reached the front door and it slid open. In they walked. The home was bright and clean, but there was something ominous about the place—the shiny counters, the potted plants with leaves made of cloth. His mother wasn't coming out.

It smelled like a hospital. They followed a woman, Sally, to a door where Sally punched in a security code, as if the door led to an airport jetway. After walking two hallways they came to his mother's room. It was small, but big enough for a bed, a desk, a dresser. David felt incredibly sad, and worse still because his mother so quietly accepted her fate. David lifted the suitcase onto the desk. The case was heavy, dense as a bookbag. With the added exertion, he had to gasp for air.

"It's okay," his father whispered in his ear.

Framed photos half filled the suitcase—the photos were suggested by the home—and David placed the frames on every available surface. He hung a few on the hooks left by the last inmate. The photos showed his mother as a younger woman. There were several of David, and a few of the whole family together. There were two of Cory, and David put them up without looking too closely.

His father unpacked his mother's clothes, a task David was happy to avoid. He didn't want to handle his mother's intimate things. Of course, there was no underwear. Diapers, his father had mentioned, were provided by the home, their cost added to the monthly fee.

David stopped to look at his mother. She sat on the bed, said nothing, hardly moved. Part of him wanted her to scream out in rage. The other part hoped she didn't really understand what was happening.

"Maybe you want to wait at the car," his father said to him. "After you say your goodbyes to your mother."

Thirty years, David thought. *Thirty years till I end up here. I better start living.* He sat next to his mother, hugged her, awkward at first, and then she draped her arm over his shoulder. He'd always had this idea of himself as a dutiful and helpful son, and now he felt the futility of it.

"Bye, Mom," he said. "See you soon."

"Fuck it," she said.

III

THE PHONE CALL rocked her from sleep. For a moment she didn't know where she was and then she did: in bed, beside David. She knew from the ring it was Marty calling.

"I've got to take this," she said.

"Sure," he replied.

She grabbed the phone and headed into his sparse bathroom. He had one towel. It was white, twisted over the rack. Men did things like that—went to the store and bought only one white towel.

"Hey," she said into the phone.

"Did I wake you?" Marty asked.

"Yeah." Even this little bit of truth felt like a lie. And it was a lie. She told herself this, if for no other reason than to keep her bearings.

"I guess it's late there."

"I guess."

"Okay," he said. "Look, I'll be brief. I'm calling to ask you to come home."

"Is something wrong?"

"I just got this big case, we're about to enter negotiations, and Kevin, he's a lot of work, and, well, I could use the help."

"Just give Elda some extra hours," she said. It was the L.A. way. If you didn't have time to spend with your family, you paid someone else to do it.

"It's just a lot of work, you know?"

"I do," she said. She had once convinced herself he was a good father, but really it all fell to Carolyn. Marty didn't even bother to sign Kevin up for sports. He didn't like to be inconvenienced.

"I know it's work," she told him. "I do it all the time."

"Yeah, but Carolyn, my job, I make a lot more—"

"This isn't about whose job pays more. It's about you looking after your son for a couple weeks while I help out my mother."

"Where are you? You sound like you're in a tin can."

"The bathroom," she said. She added, "I don't want my mother to hear."

She heard him sigh. They both knew she would give in.

"I'll be there as soon as I can," she said.

IV

It was like all the other law offices in all the other towns that David had visited: muted colors, stained wood, thick, sound-absorbing carpet. Nothing too bright or loud for the law. He wondered what ever had made him go into this business. He couldn't remember, exactly. He'd always been a good student, able to write papers and take tests, at the top of his class. What worried him were his abilities in the real world. Perhaps he'd settled on law because it seemed the career that was most like school.

"Are you sure you want to do this?" Peter Bergen asked. They were seated in his office. David glanced out the window, south, toward downtown.

"Yes, I'm sure."

"I checked your references. Everybody loves you. And we could use an estate attorney. But you're the first person

76

we've talked to about a position, let alone the first person we've considered hiring, who'd have to move here to take the job. That just doesn't happen. You're going to have to convince me that you want to move back to Detroit. Most important, convince me that you'll stay."

"It's a crazy idea," David said. "I was twelve years old the last time this city was on an upswing. It's been going downhill for years, but I want to be back. For me, this is the only real place."

"Real place?" Bergen asked.

"Yes," David said. "Real. This is the place where I first knew my family, where I learned what the seasons are, where I first felt the cold, the true cold, the cold that makes your nose crinkle and your spit bounce. Also the heat, and the sucking sound that car tires make on asphalt in the summer heat that seems impossible in a place that can get so cold. I learned to ride a bike here, to throw a ball and to catch one. This is where I got my heart broken by every sports team, over and over. I had my first kiss here, fell in love for the first time, and now I'm back because I want to be back and I don't give a damn about how the city has gone down the tubes or its poor prospects for the future. I'm connected here. It's home."

He waited for Bergen's response. He'd said more than he'd meant to say, but he was tired of everyone trashing Detroit.

Bergen seemed lost in thought.

"*You* know what I'm talking about," David said. "You've never left."

Bergen smiled. "Hell," he said. "The Tigers might even make the playoffs this year."

"I wouldn't get your hopes up."

Bergen stood, and David with him. "I'll get you an offer letter," Bergen said.

"I'll be giving up partnership," said David. "You'll need to replace it."

"You expect to be hired as a partner?"

"I expect a foot in the door, yes."

"That's more than a foot in the door."

"I'm just saying that there's a market for my labor. I ask that you pay the going rate."

*　*　*

WITHIN A WEEK he'd met with the other three partners, negotiated a small partnership stake (though without his name on the door), and begun to look for a place to live. He visited a dozen houses that managed to make Denver homes look expensive, but buying seemed too big a step, so he called his landlord and offered to continue on a month-to-month basis. The man sounded as if he might shout out a cry of joy.

There was also the delicate situation of extracting himself from his current firm. He called Tom Cutter and explained that he was simply sick about it but he had to withdraw from the firm and move back to Detroit, that filial duty and responsibility demanded it.

"Ah, David," Cutter said. "I'm really sorry. Detroit? What are you going to do for work?"

"I'll find something."

"You know anything about bankruptcy law?"

"You're saying I can't make a living planning for death in Detroit?"

Cutter wished him luck.

•   •   •

HE CALLED STACY. They had dated for almost a year, more off than on. He wasn't sure how long it had been since he'd called her. Three weeks? Four?

"I'd just stopped wondering if you were ever going to call again," she said.

"I'm not," he told her. He used fewer than twenty words to give her the story.

"Well, I hope you find what you're looking for."

"Who says I'm looking for anything?"

"Oh, please," she said.

•   •   •

HE WAS DRIVING when Carolyn called. He wasn't expecting it.

"Where are you?" she wanted to know.

"On my way home," he said.

"I'm at your apartment," she said.

He found her sitting in her rental car, a Mazda. It wasn't long till they lay shoulder-to-shoulder on their backs, the air redolent with her smell. In the dim light he could see the steady rise and fall of her breasts, hear the faint rustle of her breathing.

"I'm not staying."

"I know," he said.

"Okay, then." She sighed. She rolled to him, took him in her hands. "Can we do something about this?" she asked.

"Perhaps."

"Try harder."

He responded, though it took what seemed to him a long time, so that when it was over he didn't want to move a muscle. She reached toward the nightstand for her phone.

"You're making a call?" he asked.

"Setting the alarm."

An hour later, it woke him. She rose and dressed without saying a word. He wanted to ask her to stay but knew she wouldn't. She seemed intent on leaving.

"Goodbye, Carolyn," he said.

Through the dim light he saw her hesitate, and then perhaps she gave him a nod. When the door closed he felt his stomach clench. He thought about her as he tried to drift back to sleep.

. . .

HE WOKE TO the dawn. Muted light was making an end run around the blinds. He had a brief, fleeting memory of

Cory, of a morning when the light in the bedroom had been just like this and Cory had come in, seven or eight years old, and tapped an index finger on David's forehead. "The day is wasting away," he said, one of David's lines.

The bed smelled of Carolyn. He found his cell phone and called her, but the call went to voicemail. He rose and stripped the bed, stuffed the sheets in the little stacked washer/dryer unit. He hated housework. He hated that she was gone. He waited an hour and phoned her again, and again got voicemail. His stomach cramped and roiled on the instant coffee. It was early, but he called her mother's house.

"She's left already, David," Tina said. She had recognized him just from his voice.

"For the airport?"

"Yes, of course."

He was reminded of when Natalie left for college.

"I was going to say goodbye."

"Interesting," Tina said. She agreed to pass his message along. He saw that he was being silly, but he didn't care.

V

THE TERMINAL WAS new, with high ceilings and wide hallways, unlike the old claustrophobic tunnels where the airlines other than Northwest conducted their business. In her youth, Carolyn remembered, Northwest had been called Northwest Orient, a name that conjured up the allure of travel, the idea that you could leave Detroit and go someplace completely foreign, even exotic. Of course, the world was smaller now; in her youth California would have been exotic rather than home. Part of her looked forward to getting back. She wanted to see Kevin; she didn't want to think about herself. She was worn out with the consideration of her own problems.

She passed two stores selling athletic apparel, one green and white for Michigan State, the other blue and gold for the University of Michigan. She stopped at the latter and bought Kevin a blue hooded sweatshirt, two T-shirts, and a Nerf football. Even at Detroit Metro the souvenirs weren't from the city, except in the check-in hall, where there were new cars on display, just as there had always been.

She slowed to look as she passed the concessions, but she couldn't eat. It seemed a metaphor for everything that lay ahead. She had to act and she couldn't act. She couldn't stay with Marty and she couldn't break up the family. Worst of all, she saw that she'd done it to herself, that she'd made the deal with Marty because she thought it was what she wanted. She'd been wrong.

She had met him at a bad time in her life, after she'd broken up with a man she'd thought "the one." She and this man had spent three blissful months together, and then he informed her that his ex-girlfriend was pregnant. "I don't want to lose you," he told Carolyn, but in the end he went back to the other woman. Months later she met Marty. He pursued her relentlessly, and he was so clumsy at it that she assumed he'd never tried that hard before. It was flattering. He was a lawyer, and unlike almost every other man she'd met in Los Angeles, he had no secret dream to make movies. He lived in the real world. He felt solid and safe. She didn't think he would ever hurt her. She thought she could make a life with him, and fill in the missing pieces later.

.   .   .

"CAROLYN?" SAID A voice. She looked over. It took her a moment, but then she recognized Suzy Maxwell. It had been twenty-five years, perhaps twenty-five pounds, but this was unmistakably Suzy Maxwell, same blue eyes, same dark hair; still, something was a little different.

"Suzy?" Carolyn asked.

"It's the nose," she whispered. They were sitting one seat apart in a long row of connected chairs. "I had it done."

"Oh," Carolyn said, surprised by Suzy's line. It was the way people talked in L.A. "It looks good," Carolyn added.

"Are you okay?" Suzy asked.

"Yes, why?"

"You look upset."

"I don't like flying," Carolyn said.

They spent twenty-five seconds on the last twenty-five years. It was all they needed. At this spot, at this time, what had happened in those twenty-five years didn't matter nearly as much as the shared experiences that had come before it. Suzy lived in Encino with her two kids. She "didn't really" work; the ex-husband took care of the bills.

"So," Suzy said, "you going to the reunion?"

"What reunion?"

"Twenty-five years, our class. It's Thanksgiving weekend, this year."

"I'm not in touch with anyone," Carolyn said.

"Well, now you're in touch with me."

"I don't know," Carolyn said.

"What's wrong?" Suzy asked again. "There is obviously something wrong."

"I lost my sister," she said. "And my brother."

"I didn't know you had a brother."

Carolyn explained. She'd been working very hard to move on, but suddenly the loss of Natalie hit her. It wasn't right. Natalie deserved to live. She wasn't a twin, but Natalie's life was the one life most like her own. Natalie was the one other person she might have been. And now she was dead. There was a basic injustice to it, this random violence. You lived your life and then all of a sudden—

"I'm so sorry," Suzy said.

"And then there's my marriage," Carolyn said.

"What about it? Is he cheating?"

"Oh, no. No. At least, I don't—no. He's not cheating. *I'm* cheating."

"Oh."

"I cheated. I'm not cheating now. At least, I'm going to

stop." She thought for a moment. She hadn't cheated for almost nine hours.

"I don't know what to say about your sister or your brother, but with your marriage? I've been there," Suzy said. "Try to work it out. And don't tell your husband about the other guy."

"Okay." Carolyn felt calmer. It helped that it was Suzy, a stranger she trusted. Pam and Carrie, her best friends in L.A.—she wasn't sure she could admit her infidelity to them.

"Go to therapy. Get him to go. Work on it. For the boy, if nothing else."

"Of course," Carolyn said.

Over the loudspeaker the gate agent promised that the plane would be boarding shortly.

"You think I can make it work?" Carolyn said.

"Are you sure you really want to know what I think?" Carolyn did.

"I don't think you'll work it out. You get to a point, it's probably not going to get better. But you've got to try. You have to so you can move on without dying from guilt. It's a killer, that guilt."

The announcement came to board the plane.

"C'mon," Suzy said. "Let's get the hell out of Detroit."

. . .

THEY TOOK OFF and banked west. Carolyn could see I-94, the plane ascending just north of it, then over the Romulus

City Cemetery. The landscape, a dozen shades of green in summer, looked lush and inviting, so different from the arid parts of the West. Small droplets of water streamed across the window as the engines strained as they continued to rise.

Natalie and Dirk had died together, and it occurred to her now that she was alive because she'd been absent. She was always absent, had absented herself from the family as a reflex, and she couldn't say why. She knew only that it was foolish. She loved her sister, and if Natalie felt so strongly about Dirk, then Carolyn knew she would have, too. They were her people and she felt guilty to be alive, for had she been a good sister, she would have been with them.

VI

HE DROVE EAST, across the endless plains. Carolyn wouldn't take his calls. She was gone and David found himself sick with longing for her. He remembered odd physical details: the turquoise vein that jumped across the crook in her arm, the pink color she painted her toenails, the bony knobs at the edges of her wrists. He understood it was a silly youthful crush—he couldn't ever rule out that it was related to Natalie, to what he'd lost, most specifically his youth—but he felt it deeply. He saw no reason why even at his age he shouldn't be able to fall in love. And maybe this time enjoy it.

He drove into town on the new 696 and exited at Telegraph. He'd been driving since Colorado, two days of inter-
states, and now finally he'd made it to surface streets. He
was coming home. In the back of his car he had eight suits,
the uniform of his work. Things were still slightly formal
here. The rest of his clothes were back there, too, plus a
few books, a pair of ski boots, two diplomas, five years
of tax returns, a nine-by-twelve-inch envelope filled with
pictures of Julie and—mostly—Cory. Back in Denver he
hadn't been able to throw these pictures away, though he
found them too painful to look at. He doubted he would
ever look at them again, or let them go.

His entire life fit easily in the back of an Audi A6. He
lacked a drive for acquisition but always had the feeling
that he should have more and want more.

•   •   •

HE DROVE UP Telegraph and remembered a day in Denver
when it was gray and windy like this. Cory had had a Little League game. He was ten or eleven. They drove all the
way to a field in Arvada, the first to arrive. Soon it became
clear they would be the only ones to arrive. It was April,
cold, maybe forty degrees, the wind whipping along the
foothills, picking up dust and throwing it across the infield
the way breakers threw mist. David phoned the coach.

"Didn't you check the website? The game's called," the
coach said.

"For what?"

"Too damn cold and windy."

In Michigan, in April, you played no matter the weather. You played if it wasn't snowing or raining too hard, and you thanked God for the chance. David closed the phone, told his son the news. He got Cory to throw for ten minutes because he thought there were important lessons in it. Soon Cory's cheeks turned red and raw in the wind, and often they had to stop throwing to turn away from the flying dust. Still, they played. David could see that Cory wasn't having a good time, and that was perhaps the point. David believed in perseverance.

"I've played in worse than this," he told his son when they stopped. He handed Cory a cloth handkerchief, which he carried because the kid's nose never stopped running.

Cory blew his nose as a blanket of dust fell on them. "Maybe I won't ever have to," he said. "I could get lucky."

David made all the lights up Telegraph till he got to Maple. It was November, the day of the midterm election. He'd voted early in Colorado, a last vote in the West. The trees were bare, the Detroit sky low and gray, the air above freezing but damp, cold and familiar, again the weather of home.

• • •

On his third day at work, a Thursday, Smalls stepped into his office with the folder. David had so far billed three and a half hours, all of it for existing clients. Smalls was, appropriately, a short man, plump, in his midfifties at least, but he walked with a bounce in his step that had caught David's eye; he half expected the man to break into a foxtrot as he stepped down the halls of Bergen Smalls Rand and Bergen.

"I've got one for you," Smalls said. He set the file on an empty portion of David's desk. The other partners had been bringing by their detritus for two days, small issues that they didn't want to deal with or for which they had too little time, all of it related to estate planning. David was still making phone calls west, seeing what business he could hang on to.

"What is it?" David asked.

"A will, of course. Client died recently. I'm the executor, but I'm going to suggest we have you named. This is allowed for. I don't see any problems."

"Okay," David said. "Thanks."

Smalls sat at David's desk. "It's actually a bit of a famous case."

David reached for the file. Opened it. And that's when he saw Dirk's name.

"It was all over the papers—"

"I knew him," David said.

"How?"

David explained.

"Well, then," Smalls said. "I'm sure the family will be happy to deal with you."

David looked quickly through the will's beneficiaries: Shelly and Michelle Burton and someone named Marlon Booker. Natalie was nowhere in the will. Carolyn, either.

Shelly, the widow, got almost everything, which was

a government pension, the house in Detroit, so probably not worth much, its contents, the cars (an Impala and the Mercedes, which was still at the crime lab), $250 K from a life insurance policy, and everything in a UBS brokerage account, less $200,000 for Michelle and $100,000 for Marlon Booker, identified as a family friend. All in all, it was pretty straightforward, a few hours' work to separate assets and file the necessary documents with the court. David admired Dirk. Here was someone who had planned for the unthinkable.

He decided to call Shelly Burton. He'd need to meet with her to introduce himself and get her okay to do the work. He would tell her he'd known Dirk, or at least had met him once. It was an odd thing, and he wanted it to be aboveboard, this, his first work in Michigan.

. . .

"YOUR MOTHER IS having an affair," his father told him. David sat on the ancient family couch. His father had removed the plastic covers, thank God.

"Dad," David said, "Mom's incontinent. She's in the Alzheimer's ward of a nursing home." An affair? The idea was preposterous.

"I know that. I'm not saying they're sleeping together. You don't have to have sex to cheat."

David wondered if this was true. "Who is he?" he asked.

"Some big galumph. Chester Jovanovich. A Jew-hater, I bet, even before he lost his mind."

The intensity on his father's face suggested to David that the old man wanted something from him, Lord knew what. "Dad, are you jealous?"

"Hell yes, I'm jealous. You should see the way she takes care of him. Walks him around, combs his hair. She feeds him, for Chrissake."

"I see," David said. It was a small miracle, really. Lately David feared that if he lost his mind, he might turn into the kind of selfish jerk he had always hated. He found it terrifying, not being able to control who you were.

"What do you want me to do?" David asked.

"Who said I want you to do anything?"

"I guess I don't get it, Dad. It sounds like a decent situation. Mom has something to do and Chester Whateveravich has someone besides the nurses to look after him. Does he have family?"

"He's a Medicaid case, the lucky SOB"

Apparently luck, like beauty, was in the eye of the beholder.

"Don't send me to that home," his father said. "If the time comes, just grow a pair and shoot me instead."

.   .   .

MIDDLE NOVEMBER, the time of somber light. It would stay like this for months, till mid-March or so, unbroken only for the odd clear winter's day, when the temperature might drop to forty below zero even if the sky was so blue it could break your heart. There was a reason why the Swedes settled here, the Finns. Sure, the French had founded the place, leaving place-names mispronounced all over the state, but it was the others who'd cut down the forest primeval and filled the factories: Scandinavians, Eastern Europeans drifting east from Chicago, and, later, blacks coming up from the South. Now all were scattering.

It was late in the afternoon when he drove to Shelly's. She was a black woman of indeterminate middle age, tall and mildly plump with straightened hair and a gaudy wedding ring he suspected wasn't worth much. He sat in her living room, lined with bookcases, the books without their dust jackets. It was an odd touch, and it seemed to mute the room's light, just as the light outside was muted. It was a cozy room, and he felt comfortable in it.

She poured him tea and thanked him for coming. He explained that he had once met her husband. He felt a smile twisted on his face. He was nervous, though he wasn't sure why. She had that effect on him. It had something to do with her eyes, big and round and black, as if they could see through him. It was part of an idea he knew he had, namely that black people somehow had a better idea what was really going on in the world than he did. It was a silly prejudice, but he could never shake it. Odd, he thought, how hard it was to get beyond skin color.

He told himself he had nothing to worry about here. Burton's was an easy case—any new lawyer could have handled it.

"Do the Evanses have any claim on the money?" Shelly asked.

"No, Dirk left everything to you, except for portions for your daughter and someone named Marlon Booker."

"A hundred grand for Marlon," she said. He asked about Marlon. "Marlon was Dirk's nephew—not by blood. Marlon is the son of the man Dirk thought of as his brother. That was Everett, but Everett died. So now Marlon is Dirk's cross to bear."

"Any idea how I find Marlon?"

"Keep checking here. He'll come around, sooner or later."

"You sure?"

"It's part of Dirk's deal. Marlon always has a place to go. The downstairs guest room is his."

"How 'bout Marlon's mother?" David asked. Mothers tended to know how to contact their children.

"Patrice. You can ask her. I'm not sure she knows where her son is, but you can ask. If you can find her."

Shelly went to the kitchen, then returned shortly with an address book and read David the number, a 313, like everyone, whites and blacks, used to have. They spent the next ten minutes signing paperwork.

"Please, Mr. Halpert, let's get this closed up as soon as possible," she said.

"I understand."

"I want to move down to Texas, to be close to my daughter. I'm ready to list the house."

"It's a lovely home," he said, and he meant it.

"Wanna buy it?" she asked.

VII

SHE REALIZED THAT Marty was bulkier than David, slightly taller, with more hair. A happier, more satisfied version of a man. Her husband had grown up in Pasadena. He took his success in stride, something to be expected, like the pleasant weather.

The first week back Carolyn allowed herself simply to fall into routine, to spend time with Kevin and catch up at work (287 unanswered e-mails waited upon her return), and to act deliberately, without desperation. She wanted happiness, not to settle. It wouldn't be easy.

She made love with Marty the third night back. It was his idea, and she was glad for it, a way to deal with her guilt. It started after she'd put Kevin to bed and was standing at the stove, boiling water for ginger tea. Marty came up behind her and put his hand on the small of her back. "I'll be right up," she said before he could speak. She didn't want to hear him ask, "Are you coming to bed?" or "Come to bed," in that way he had. He was hopeless at flirtation, always had been. She couldn't even blame him. She'd known, and she'd looked past it, thought it wasn't important. One day she would list all the things she used to think weren't important, and in a different column those she once thought were; then she would hold the two lists together just to see all the entries on the wrong side.

Sleeping with Marty wasn't horrible, but it wasn't great. It was just one of the many things they did together because even in the absence of passion there was some force that compelled them to do this silly thing together. Once, afterward, lying next to him, she'd felt as though the next thing to do was to sign her name to something, by Marty's, as they did on their tax returns. As if to say, *There, done.*

And so it was tonight. It was the first time in a month. If she went back to David after a month, it wouldn't be like this. She was forty-two. She calculated that she made love with Marty thirty times a year—that seemed to be the pace of it—and so that at this rate, and allowing for some slowing with age, she'd sleep with him a thousand more times in the next forty-two years. The thought of forty-two more tax returns seemed far more palatable.

He was asleep. She knew this from his breathing. There was enough light in the room—from the glow of the case that housed the TV and audiovisual components, from the outdoor security lights that made it past their blackout blinds—that she could get out of bed and put on the nightgown she always left at the end of her bed, in case Kevin needed her. She decided to go to his room.

He slept in a ball, breathing deeply. She stood at his bedside, bent over at the waist, and listened to the languorous draws of breath. It was part of her routine, the way she dealt with nighttime terrors and general sleeplessness. She defied a mother to listen to her child sleep and not feel at least a small bit calmer.

At some point her back began to hurt, and so she sat by the bed, listening still. She then laid herself out next to him. Kevin's nightlight threw odd shadows on the ceiling. It was a good room. A peaceful room. It was, really, what you needed. The German car was nice, the four thousand square feet for three people, the pool, the magnolia tree trucked up from the South by the previous owner—all this was lovely, more even than her father the doctor had taught her to expect. But it wasn't necessary. What was necessary was a peaceful room for your child.

·   ·   ·

Suzy Maxwell called the next week, a half hour before Carolyn had to leave for therapy.

"Thought any more about the reunion?" Suzy wanted to know.

"No," Carolyn said. "Not one bit."

"Things really are bad, aren't they? I can hear it in your voice."

"Really, Suzy, I just can't deal with the reunion. I mean—"

"I just called to see how you're doing."

"Why?"

"At the airport? You looked so sad. It's made me think about you."

"I'm frozen," Carolyn said. "Can't go forward, can't go back. I can barely acknowledge my husband. He knows something's up and has chosen to try to ignore it. I can see that. I guess he thinks it'll pass. But it's not passing. I've made myself literally sick to my stomach. I can barely eat."

"You should get help. Professional help."

"I've got a therapy appointment in thirty minutes," Carolyn said. "I've got to go, but listen, I appreciate the call."

"So you're getting help. That's good."

Out the window of her office, Carolyn could see a bank of clouds rolling in. Below, a light turned red on Wilshire, and then the street lit up with brakelights. She told Suzy goodbye and left the office, far earlier than she really needed to, but that was okay. She figured it was about time she showed up for something early.

.   .   .

THAT NIGHT SHE put Kevin to bed by reading him *The Sneetches*. He was a little old for the story, they both knew this, but it was something they had between them, a ritual of connection. She could recite the book by heart. The book itself was old and fragile, the aqua dust jacket ripped, the cloth cover worn, its corners rounded with use. It had been Carolyn's book when she was a girl, and Natalie's before that, a favorite of their mother's because, Carolyn used to think, "sneetches" sounded like a German word.

She finished reciting and closed the book, careful to hold it together. Kevin looked at her. He was a gorgeous boy, with large, dark eyes and black bangs. Obviously he had his father's coloring, but his face, with those big cheeks and pointy chin, came from the Evanses.

"What is it, Mom?" he asked.

She realized what she was doing: she was dividing up

the marriage, right down to parsing out what part of her child belonged to which side. Thin wrists: Evans. Thick fingers: Clearwater. Long legs: Evans. Smile: Clearwater.

"Are you ready for some sleepies?" she asked.

"Sleepies, Mom? What am I, six years old?"

"You're my boy," she said. "And you used to love that word."

"Yeah, like when I was young."

She smiled at him and turned out the light.

• • •

SHE SPENT THE week trying to make it work with Marty, hiring a sitter so they could go to a movie, dinner. Once she made him eggs for breakfast, a special treat after he'd been instructed to watch his cholesterol. She knew he noticed the change, but he said nothing. Just as he had waited out her bad behavior, he tried to silently enjoy the good. He wasn't a man to bring things to a head.

And then she starting feeling sick in the mornings. She knew what it was. This was the third time she'd been pregnant. She'd miscarried once and had Kevin, both with Marty.

In the past she and Marty had had fertility testing, and it turned out that Marty wasn't all that fertile and that his chemistry didn't mix particularly well with hers. No surprise there, she thought in the doctor's office. The two previous pregnancies had been accomplished artificially. Eventually she and Marty stopped using birth control and she never got pregnant. She had been careful with David, but—well, it had to be him.

She called her therapist, Mandy, made an appointment, and picked up the phone to call David. Then she thought better of it. She didn't know what she wanted yet, and she still had a little time.

The mornings were hell, but later in the day she felt better. The truth was that she wanted another child. She hadn't realized this, but she knew it now, now that it was not only possible but happening.

It was Friday, the traffic brutal as she inched her way home, though she'd now have two days off and time to think. Then, next week, she'd make a decision. It was a relief, really, just to be determined to decide, even if she wasn't sure what the decision should be. Afterward she could get on with life without having to think about herself all the time. She was sick of that.

She walked in the house and found Marty sitting in the front hallway chair, a chair where no one ever sat, where coats were thrown when they entertained and it was cool enough in L.A. to wear a coat. She saw he had her cell phone in his hand. She had mistakenly left it at home that morning.

"Who's David?" he asked.

"David who?"

"David. He called you. He said he was a friend from Michigan."

Christ, she thought.

"Who is he?" Marty demanded.

"We need to talk," she said.

1994

I

His mother said his father was waiting for him.

"What I do?" Marlon asked. He'd just walked in the house. He was supposed to be home by six. His digital watch said 5:51.

"He just wants to see you."

The old man—that's how he looked—was propped up on the couch, leaning on the pillows and covered in blankets. He lifted a shaky arm to point the remote and mute the TV. Skin hung from his upper arm where there had once been muscle.

"Hey," Marlon said.

"How was school?"

"Good."

"Not so good, huh?" his father said. "You don't much like school."

Marlon wondered, *What kind of trap is this?*

"It was never much my favorite," said his father. "But I wish I'd tried harder and gone to college. Coulda stayed out of East Side Steel that way."

Marlon couldn't get over that his father had lost all of his hair, and all that weight. His eyes were sunken in his head, not that Marlon could really look. He caught short glimpses, from the side; it was all he could take.

"The chemo sucks," his father said.

"It's like that's what's making you sick."

"Feels like it. Maybe you could do me a favor."

"What?" Marlon asked.

"Two things. First, I think I could eat something maybe. Could you make me some toast, with just a little butter?"

"Toast?" Marlon asked. He liked toast, made it for himself.

"Yeah, toast."

"Okay. I can do toast."

"And there's the other thing," Everett said.

Marlon waited.

"Once in a while, call me Dad."

Okay, Marlon thought. Call him Dad. He'd have to concentrate on that. For some reason, "Dad" didn't come out naturally.

He went out to the kitchen and got the bread. He picked rye, his father's favorite. "He wants toast," he explained to his mother. She nodded, as if she had known it all along. He dropped the toast into the toaster and waited for the bread to turn brown. Then he spread a little butter on it and took it out to the living room, smelling that distinct scent of rye. His father straightened up, took a bite, then another. He chewed slowly. Marlon could hear the crunching; it made the skin on his arms crawl.

It didn't take long, less time than it took to make the toast. "Pass me the bucket," his father said. Those two bites came right back up. His father wiped his mouth with the handkerchief he kept for that purpose.

"I'm sorry, son," he said. "It's good toast, but I don't think I'm going to be able to eat it."

"Shit, Dad," Marlon said.

II

"MILES ZANE HAS dropped off the face of the earth," said McMahon.

It had been a couple weeks since they'd heard from Miles, but Dirk doubted that he'd fled. Miles might have been *in* the earth, or, more likely, he was spooked and lying low. Dirk said this to McMahon. McMahon was old school, also just old, tall, still in pretty good shape; he had a certain type of old white-guy style. He got a haircut every Saturday, a manicure every other. Dirk had made a study of such things, the habits of the powerful.

"I'm thinking, this is my chance for a graceful exit from

undercover work," Dirk said. "Hell, Miles was questioning my age. And he was right. It's a young man's game. I've had to start dying my hair."

"I don't have anybody better than you," McMahon said. He sat on the edge of Dirk's desk, smiling as if it hurt. Dirk was fairly certain McMahon was studying his hair. He wished he hadn't mentioned the dye. It was like exposing a wound.

"I knew this day would come," McMahon said.

"What day?"

"The day you wanted a desk job."

"Did I say anything about a desk job?"

"I'm sixty-four years old, Dirk. Next year they force me out." He paused. "How would you feel about my desk?"

"How would I feel about it? As in, how would I feel about sitting behind it and running the office?"

McMahon nodded.

"I'll have to think about that," Dirk said, a little flabbergasted, both by the honor and by the burden. He could think of a handful of guys, all older, all white, who wanted the job and were ahead of him in line. He mentioned two of them.

"Good men," McMahon said. "Also, no geniuses. And with what's going on in this city, we need brains."

"Any city," Dirk said.

"You been out to Dearborn lately?" McMahon asked.

He had. Dearborn, the home of Ford and Arabic street signs. Not many brothers out there, which, of course, had always been old man Ford's design. Keeping Arabs out had probably never occurred to him.

"One of the guys that tried to blow up the World Trade Center last year, his whole family lives out there. Mother, father, three sisters, uncles, aunts, you name it. We need the kind of work you do, and I don't see Kreiler or Jurgys running the Arab special agents we're going to have to find. And you might like it, management. You could stop dyeing your hair."

"I don't like wearing suits," Dirk said. He was stalling, trying to think it through. If he got the job, there'd be a lot of pissed-off white guys. His pay would go up. His hours would be normal.

"You look good in a suit." McMahon stood up from his desk. "How 'bout putting Miles Zane away, and we'll make a change. I'll start grooming you myself."

"We don't even know where Miles is," Dirk said.

"He'll turn up," McMahon said. "You said so yourself."

.   .   .

NATALIE CALLED TO say she was engaged, so Dirk drove out to Bloomfield Hills to have dinner with her at their mother's. It was a last-minute thing on a school night; Shelly had decided that Michelle should stay home. Shelly was cool toward Dirk's white family; she felt they didn't pay him the proper respect, the short notice of this invitation being just the latest evidence. Dirk had to make a choice, so he told his mother he would come without his wife and daughter. Going alone seemed the best way to keep everyone happy, or at least not terribly unhappy. He figured within a family like his you couldn't ask for more.

Bloomfield Hills was like a different country. No, Dirk decided, it was more than that. Travel across the river to Windsor, Ontario, and it seemed more like Detroit than Bloomfield, with all the big trees and clean streets, gas that cost forty cents more a gallon, and plenty of luxury German and Japanese cars. Of course none of the Bloomfield doctors and lawyers had dark-tinted windows or twenty-inch wheels.

His mother lived on a road off Lone Pine, which was 17 Mile. Ten miles from his house, and also light-years away. This was a neighborhood of Colonial homes and newer McMansions. What was left of the forest primeval was in its full glory, magnificent trees that threw shade across the streets. He didn't notice the cop till the guy tweaked his siren.

There were two ways to play it. One, show him the FBI badge when he came up, or two, play dumb till things got further along. Dirk decided on the latter. He wasn't in a hurry.

"License and registration, proof of insurance," said the cop. Not even a "please." He was pasty white and young, maybe not yet thirty. Dirk had papers in the name of Barry Stevens and Dirk Burton, the latter hidden. He fished them out from under the seat.

The cop retreated, sat in his car, then returned and handed everything back. "Mr. Burton, where are you going?"

"Perhaps first you'd tell me why you stopped me."

"You were driving suspiciously."

That was a new one. "Can you explain?" Dirk asked.

"I did."

"You had no probable cause."

"Like I said," said the kid. "You were driving odd."

Dirk held up his badge and the kid actually stepped back. "I think," Dirk said, "that you didn't like the look of my car, and that you stopped me without probable cause, and that all I have to do to get you in a whole lot of trouble is to make a phone call from my office."

The cop considered this. Finally he said, "What do you want?"

"I want you to ask me to let you go," Dirk said.

"What?"

"Say, 'I'm sorry, sir, I made a mistake. Would you let me off this one time? I won't do it again.' "

It was as if the cop wanted to speak but couldn't.

"And it would be good if you begged a little, you know?" Dirk suggested. "So you sound contrite."

"I don't have to put up with this," said the cop.

"No, but consider the consequences of not putting up with it."

It was a calculation black people made all the time; without the badge, Dirk would be making it at this very moment. He could see the young cop struggling to come to the obvious conclusion. "I made a mistake," he said finally. "Please, would you let me off this one time, please?"

Dirk liked the extra "please." "Okay," he said, "but don't let me again catch you pulling over a brother for no reason."

The cop stared. Dirk could feel the hatred, which was some small comfort. This wasn't the first time he'd given a white cop a hard time. It was never as satisfying as he hoped.

"For the record," Dirk said, "I'm going to see my mother."

. . .

DESPITE THE STOP, he got to the house early. His mother wasn't home, Natalie wasn't there, but Arthur, his mother's husband, came out to meet him in the driveway. Dirk was shocked, Arthur looked so frail, ghostly. He had colon cancer, and it obviously wasn't going well. He wore khakis cinched tight and a T-shirt that hung on his shoulders as it would have on a wire hanger.

"You look bigger every time I see you," Arthur said.

"You know, Arthur, that's not something you say to a man who's forty," Dirk said.

"C'mon inside."

They sat in the kitchen, as they always did. It was odd, because the rest of the house was so nice. Perhaps when you got to a certain level of opulence you desired less. Arthur wanted to know details of the drug trade. He read articles in medical journals about the effects of crack and crystal meth. He knew the science of it, but it was the social aspects that interested him.

"Well, I'm getting out of the risk-your-life business," Dirk said.

"You're quitting the FBI?"

"No, just undercover work. It's a young man's game."

"Life is a young man's game." Arthur asked about Shelly and Michelle. Dirk talked for a while, thinking he could really use a beer. Finally he asked for one.

"Good idea." Arthur started to get up, but Dirk held him in place with an upraised palm. He went to the refrigerator, opened the stainless steel door, and found two St. Pauli Girls.

"So you're marrying off Natalie," Dirk said.

"Just in time."

Dirk heard the wrong tone in his voice, just as he had when he had talked to Natalie. He sat down with the beers.

"You don't sound any more sure of it than Natalie does."

Arthur attempted a smile.

His mother arrived almost forty-five minutes late. "So tell me everything," she said.

He always felt the mystery of his life most when he was with his mother. He hadn't forgiven her, exactly, because he couldn't understand why she'd done what she'd done. He knew she believed her actions were justified, and this softened things, even if it didn't make them clear. When he thought of Michelle he couldn't imagine letting someone else raise his child, and yet both of his parents had made that choice. "Don't spend your life waiting for Tina to get in touch with her feelings," Natalie had advised, and that deepened the mystery, because Nat seemed to be angrier with their mother than Dirk, as though she couldn't forgive her mother for keeping her.

"It's really too bad Michelle and Shelly couldn't come," Tina said. "I haven't seen Michelle for ages."

Give me more than a five-hour notice, he thought, but he held it in. He smiled. White people, he knew, liked to see him smile.

III

MARLON WAS THINKING of Z. He got the cancer, and they radiated the stuffing out of him, till that bushy 'fro melted right off his head and his skin started to look like rolling paper, the burned kind right before it disintegrates. No one in the neighborhood knew what to do. You felt bad for the guy, but going to his house and sitting with him while he looked so bad and couldn't do anything was like dying yourself. Z's mom was grateful when Marlon came, and this made it even worse, on account of how she'd hated the old neighborhood crew every second that Z had been healthy.

But then Z got a little better and one afternoon his mother let him out. Marlon was there, and Eric, and Ricky

Spooner. They all walked down to Eric's house, four doors away but like a mile for Z. Z said he weighed fifty-eight pounds. They were all twelve then. Eric produced a joint.

"Try this," he said. "Makes you want to eat."

It was offered around and no one would take it, so Eric lit the joint himself and took a hit. "Jesus," he said. "Ain't gonna kill you. Gonna be sick, might as well be high."

It was solid logic, Marlon thought. Z tried the joint and had a coughing fit. It spoke to his evident frailty that no one laughed at him. Eric even coached him on what to do. Z tried a second time and was able to hold down some smoke. From that point on he smoked regularly. And he got better.

Marlon figured he had to try the same thing for his father. He had to do something. He couldn't just watch his father fade away. There was irony in this, because all along he'd been wishing his father would get off his case and now the old man was too weak to do anything but sit on the couch, and it was still no good. It made Marlon wonder if you didn't need the push-back, if life meant nothing without the resistance.

One thing he knew: it felt good to make his father smile.

He packed a joint in a chewing tobacco can, slipped it into his pocket, and went downstairs to the living room. It was just after school, the time he normally hung in the neighborhood while his mother was still at work.

"Yo, Dad. Come sit with me in the back yard."

"On the grass?"

"I'll get the folding chairs," Marlon said.

"Why?"

"Can you just do it?"

Marlon waited, watching his father decide. At first Marlon thought he was deciding if he would go to the back yard; then Marlon realized his father was deciding if he *could* go. "Help me up," he said. He reached out and Marlon tugged him to his feet. He was still heavy, but unsteady now.

Outside there were royal blue streaks between the clouds. Marlon liked that kind of sky, one that had everything in it. "I'm cold," his father said.

"Here, sit here." Marlon helped the old man into the chair, then ran off for a blanket. He returned and covered his father like a man in a barbershop. Then Marlon pulled the other chair close. They were old folding chairs, woven with frayed nylon. "Okay, Dad," Marlon said. "I got something for you."

"What is it?" his father asked.

"Gonna make you feel better," Marlon said.

"You're doing better in school?"

Marlon turned his hand over, showing the can. Then he twisted off the top and there was the joint, speckled with a couple flecks of chew dust.

"What the hell are you doing?" his father said.

"I got this for you, Dad."

"I forbid you to smoke it."

"It's for you. It'll be good for you. Zeke Taylor, when he got the cancer, he was just like you, puking his guts out, but then he got some smoke and he was better. Put on some LBs and everything. You seen him. He's better."

His father stared at the can, then looked at Marlon. Their eyes met, and Marlon realized he hadn't looked his father in the eye for a long time. They were watery, the eyes of a man in pain.

"C'mon, Dad. Try it."

"I've got lung cancer and you want me to smoke?"

"If you could drink it, I'da brought you a bottle."

"What I'd really like is a real cigarette," the old man said.

"Don't be stupid, Dad."

He took the joint. Marlon handed him a pack of matches, the kind with an advertisement for night school on the inside.

"I don't want you doing this."

"This ain't about me," Marlon said.

His father lit up, inhaled, then coughed. Marlon laughed. He couldn't help it—it was funny. Then his father laughed. When had they last laughed together? His father took another hit.

That night they had grilled cheese. Once his father had stopped eating, Marlon's mother had stopped cooking, but on this night the old man ate everything. Marlon watched him shovel it in. At one point his father looked up and winked at Marlon. Marlon smiled, but then looked down. There was only so long he could look his father in the eye.

IV

MILES WANTED TO meet at Nemo's. He'd resurfaced, just as McMahon predicted. Dirk didn't see any harm in Nemo's: lots of people and close to the office, easy to have backup around. And not the kind of place anyone would plan an ambush.

He was driving there when Natalie called him on his real cell phone.

"Thought you might want to know, my dad's in the hospital."

"Serious?"

"Yes. Something turned. Not the right way, obviously."

"When did he go in?" Dirk asked.

"Yesterday."

"Why didn't you call me?"

"What were you going to do?" she asked.

"Go visit him."

"It's too late tonight. He's in the ICU. They're strict."

"I can get in," Dirk told her.

"I saw the will today. You're in it. Thought you should know."

"Wow," Dirk said. "That's nice of him."

"You're equal with Carolyn and me."

It seemed impossible that this could be right. Carolyn and Natalie were Arthur's daughters, his flesh and blood. Dirk wasn't supposed to be an heir.

"Why would he do that?"

"For Mom," Natalie said. "And he said it was time someone did you a favor. You're going to get about a half-million bucks."

He almost drifted off the road. It was an impossible number. He'd worked long enough that he could already get a pension. And with this he could stop working altogether. He pulled the car over on Michigan Avenue.

"You going to say anything?" Natalie asked.

"I've pulled over now, but I still don't know what to say."

"There will be more when Mom dies, if she doesn't spend it all."

"Man, Natalie."

"You don't sound happy."

"Happy that Arthur is dying?"

"Happy that he's treating you like a son."

Dirk thought of the times he'd been places where people were rich and white together, how easy it all felt. It made sense now. He imagined what he'd tell Shelly when he got home tonight. He'd wake her and tell her, and she would cry. He knew this. He felt he could almost cry himself.

"I don't deserve it," he told Natalie.

"Don't be an idiot," she said.

. . .

NEMO'S WAS A white-guy place, a sports bar founded in 1965 and still on Michigan Avenue, just down from Tiger Stadium. There were photos on the walls of old sports heroes of Detroit's past. Bobby Layne, Gordie Howe, Al

Kaline. Dirk found Miles in the bar watching a college football preview show on ESPN, the sound off.

"You must have played," Dirk said, his way of saying
hello. Dirk had played in high school and could usually
recognize old members of the football brotherhood.

"Never much liked it, so I quit. High school coach was
all over me, but it wasn't me." He looked over at Dirk.
"Getting beat up for no good reason."

"Pros make a few bucks."

"Short careers," Miles said.

An interesting observation from a drug dealer. Dirk
pulled out a kilo of heroin, wrapped up like a present.
There was even a little blue ribbon.

"Happy birthday," he said to Miles.

An envelope was suddenly resting on Dirk's thigh. He
took it and slid it into the breast pocket of his jacket, sure
that it would get caught on tape.

"Easy there," Miles said. "Let's not broadcast it."

They sat for a moment in silence. Miles was to test the
kilo. If all went well, next week he'd say he wanted five.
Actually, he'd be followed and arrested before he could
even cut it.

The money in Dirk's pocket had to be lighter than the
heroin had been, but it felt like a hundred pounds. "You
ever wanted to take it for yourself?" Everett once asked
him. "Just once?"

"No," Dirk had lied, but it wasn't a special lie. At some
point, he realized, he'd lied to everyone.

Miles rattled the ice cubes in his glass. The business was complete, caught on camera and on audiotape.

"I'm not hungry," Dirk said. "How 'bout you?"

"Naw, let's bounce."

They walked out to the awning. It was a fall evening, but Dirk thought he could pick up the scent of winter. With weather he liked extremes: the dense air of summer, humid and almost tropical, and the dry crackling cold of a winter cold snap, when the snow squeaked when you walked on it and you'd run your tongue around the inside of your mouth to warm your face. That weather was coming. By the time it got warm again he'd be wearing a suit to work and checking the balance of his pension plan. It made him a little sad, letting the undercover work go, but he just wasn't young anymore.

As he turned to say goodbye to Miles he spotted the listening van and so didn't really notice the black car till it was quite close. It was an old Lincoln, lumbering slowly on the bricks of the street, tinted glass windows, the driver's-side rear window slowly sliding down. That's when he knew. He was about two feet from Miles. He dove the other way and hid behind a parked car, his hand braced on its cold metal side panel.

Later, he told Shelly he might have been able to save Miles, that if he had just reached out and given him a shove he would have been a moving target rather than a large, stationary one. "He trafficked in heroin," she said, and this was true, but he was a man, and rather intelligent.

Dirk thought someday he might have been something. "You were going to put him in jail," Shelly reminded him, and this time he stayed silent, unable to explain himself. It was an oddity of the job, how he sometimes cared for the people he put away.

The gun was vintage, something Dirk hadn't seen since his first days at the Bureau: a .44 Auto Mag. Four shots hit Miles and, miraculously, no one else. One of those shots, the only one that counted, barely nicked Miles's aorta. Dirk crouched over him and called for an ambulance, identifying himself as an FBI agent. Other agents came running, from inside the restaurant, from the van, from the street. Miles realized he had a crowd.

"Shit," he whispered. "You a cop."

"FBI," Dirk said.

"You lied to me, Barry."

"I won't anymore," he said. In another minute the EMT guys arrived. They worked furiously at first, then started taking their time, and soon stopped trying at all. In all the years he'd been on the job, Dirk had only ever been shot at once before, and it wasn't nearly this close.

Haig was filling in tonight for McMahon. Haig would have been one of the guys pissed off by Dirk's promotion, but he had little to worry about now. Dirk told him he wanted to go home. Haig allowed it. There was plenty of paperwork to do, but they both knew it could wait. From now on Dirk was going to have ample time in the office.

Dirk found his car and sat in it for a moment. He needed a chance to breathe. Then he pulled out on Michigan Avenue and headed west toward Henry Ford Hospital. Maybe he could do something for Arthur. If nothing else, they might get a few words. Dirk could thank him, not just for the money but for what it symbolized: Arthur was telling him that he belonged, that he really was somebody's son. The very idea choked him up.

He ran into traffic and didn't want to wait, so he put the flashing light on his roof and hit the gas. He had Marvin Gaye on the stereo, the window defrost running, and a clear destination. It was late, well past visiting hours, but he had a badge, and with that they'd always let you in.

2006

I

David visited his mother once a month, though she no longer knew he was there. All her attention was focused on her new male companion.

David found her at the TV. She had been a proud woman. Now there was a quarter inch of gray hair at her scalp. There were food stains on her blouse. She didn't seem to care, or even know.

"Hey, Mom," he said. She didn't turn, didn't look up. One of her hands started to shake. She was in a wooden chair with a cushion that had a plastic cover. He knelt on one knee beside her. "Mom," he said again.

Slowly she turned her head. He smiled, but she did not. "Mom?"

"Hello," she said.

He gave it another fifteen minutes and was never sure if she knew him. He asked questions that she didn't answer and gave her news from the outside world, news that he thought might cheer her (the Democrats took control of Congress), but there was never a response. Even when he told her he was leaving she said nothing. When he stood, though, she stood. Maybe it was habit, some old connection in her head still working, and this simple act set him back. He hugged her, and took in an unpleasant smell of staleness before he said his goodbye. He turned to find a Jamaican woman to let him out, but instead there was his mother's friend, the big galumph, as his father called the man. He shuffled over to David's mother, and, still standing, she helped him to sit in her chair.

He felt an internal kick then, and damn if it didn't jab like jealousy. His father, he thought, might not be so crazy after all. He looked at his mother and her friend, but there was really nothing to be done. He turned and left.

.   .   .   .

HE DROVE SOUTH on Orchard Lake, passing one small strip mall after another. It was snowing. At Maple he headed east. He'd promised his father he'd have dinner with him. A visit to Mom at the home, dinner with Dad. This was what now constituted his Saturdays.

The snow made him think of Cory. He should never have let him go on that ski trip. Had David refused, it would have saved the boy's life. But the truth was that David had been on shaky ground; the kid had wanted to get away from him, and Julie had thought it a good idea. He couldn't blame her. There had been a time when he might have blamed her for just about everything, but never that.

He'd been working like a madman, trying to prove himself worthy of partnership, and so had brought home a stack of papers and spread them all over the ping-pong table in the basement, the only place with enough area to handle the whole case so he wouldn't have to move it at mealtime. He liked to make changes and edits by hand in blue pen, typing them later or—if he managed to be neat in his notation—giving them to his secretary. The basement was unfinished—a poured concrete floor with a drain, washing machine and dryer, a couple bare light bulbs hanging from short cords. It reminded him of places where he'd studied in college (law school had been nicer) and so in this way had some connection to his youth.

He was a workhorse, but what did he have to show for all those years of work? He was still barely able to keep ahead of the bills, his retirement account had taken a dive in the tech bust and never come back, he was working a job that was really about cheating the government out of money, which hardly seemed a worthy life calling. He wanted to get somewhere in the world, but it was obvious he had already traveled as far as he was likely to go.

He spent the better part of Saturday in the basement, then emerged in the dusky afternoon to head off to the dry cleaners and then the gym, but the dry cleaners had closed at noon (he'd thought four) and at the gym he'd barely had the energy to complete what he'd always thought of as half a workout. He'd never been a great athlete, but he'd had stamina, and took pride in it. He could be beaten on skill but never, ever outlasted.

It was an oddity that the health club occupied a space in a strip mall next to a tavern. David left the club having just showered, hair wet against the rapidly chilling air. As he walked to his car he watched a bar patron get into the car next to his, turn the engine over, and then back out while turning the wheel, so the front end of that ancient Subaru raked the entire passenger side of David's Audi, briefly lifting the right side of the car into the air.

The sound was sickening—nails on a chalkboard. David ran the last few steps to inspect his ruined car. The driver staggered to his feet shaking his head, reeking of beer.

"Dude," he said, "I'm so sorry. Really. That's the stupidest thing ever."

It was hard to argue.

The police came, made a report. "Word to the wise," the cop said. "Park at the other end of the lot. This happens more often than you would think."

He got home an hour late and Julie ripped into him, how he absented himself from the family even when he was there, and how he was literally absenting himself, working till nine at night, all day Saturday, then going out and coming back late without even having the decency to call.

He took her out to the garage. "Oh, just great," she said, as if the car were his fault. She went back inside to start the dinner.

He debated helping her, but instead went to the living room, turned on the TV, and dozed off on the couch. Cory shook him awake. Cory's friend Adam Burkley stood next to him. "Dinnertime," his son said.

The four of them ate in relative silence. Afterward the boys laid siege to the TV and Julie worked to clean the kitchen. David offered to help. "I got this," she said. There was nothing left to do but head back to the basement and try to finish the work.

Later, he realized that the ping-pong table had probably looked as chaotic to the boys as it did to him now. Papers scattered everywhere, most filled with scratches of blue ink. Worse was that not only were the papers not in any order—and reorganizing them would have taken several hours—but now many of them were wet, the notes blurred and unreadable. Pages had melted into each other. He'd started this revision after the meeting on Wednesday. He had thousands of dollars of billable hours into it.

Had it just been that—money—he probably would have exploded anyway. He had always had an ample reservoir of anger. It wasn't just the ruined work that would have to be replaced, but also the car in the garage that would need to spend two weeks in the shop; the paltry reservoir of cash at the bank and the meager long-term savings in the brokerage account, his wife, who could only find fault with him, his son, who was so careless and ungrateful. He marched into the living room and interrupted the boys watching TV.

"What happened to my papers?" he yelled.

Cory sat up. "There was an accident."

"They're ruined!"

"We put them back," Cory said.

"Do you have any idea how long I've been working on that project?" He moved closer. That's when he noticed the puzzle on the coffee table; from the box he could see it was of the famous Escher sketch of hands drawing each other. The puzzles were Julie's idea, something she and Cory could do together. Cory loved piecing together the picture, often begging his mother to join him. David moved forward and pushed the puzzle slightly, so that a small portion of the exterior—they'd fitted all the straight-edge pieces together—spilled onto the carpet.

"Dad!" Cory yelled.

"You like that? You've been working on that and then someone just wrecks it?"

Cory moved to the puzzle, but David pushed him back on the couch, surprised after it happened at just how easily the boy had been propelled backward.

"Dad, don't." Cory charged again and David reared back and hit him with a roundhouse right.

He'd used an open hand, thank God, but the blow still sent the boy flying back to the couch and brought Julie running from the kitchen. Cory was crying. Through the tears he managed to yell, "What are you doing?" Julie jumped in with the same question. David let loose a tirade. He stopped talking midsentence. He watched his wife comforting his son, and then he heard a noise. He'd forgotten about Adam, who was cowering in the reading chair. When David saw the frightened boy, he also saw himself:

an angry and bitter man incapable of enjoying the gifts before him.

This was the last week of his son's life, and David realized later that he would spend all the rest of his days wishing that he could change what had happened. That night David apologized to Cory, said that he wished he could take it back, and the boy just shrugged, as he did the rest of the week, avoiding his father whenever possible, not speaking to him. In fact, the last thing David remembered Cory saying was what he'd said that night on the couch:

"God, Dad, you're a jerk."

II

CAROLYN SAT IN her office and studied the pamphlet. "Risk Factors for Older Mothers." A man must have picked that title. Having a baby at any age was risk enough. She was probably fourteen weeks pregnant.

Carpenter stuck his head in the office. "We gotta make a move," he said. There was a meeting downtown. He was a beefy guy in his thirties, newly married, first kid on the way. She pitied him.

"Ready in a sec," she said. "Meet me in the lobby."

She knew she'd keep the baby: the thought of ending the pregnancy was worse than the thought of ending her marriage. Marty wasn't going to raise another man's child; he barely raised his own. In any case, she didn't want him involved. They'd already agreed to two weeks of keeping up appearances for Kevin and then deciding on a course of action. She was interested to know how Marty would decide, but deep down she knew she was already gone. She'd find a way to make it up to Kevin, and maybe one day he'd understand.

She pictured Carpenter pacing downstairs in the lobby, hands locked behind his back. She picked up the phone and called David.

"I'm in agony without you," he said when he picked up. Just like that, off the cuff. He was good. It was easy to see what her sister had liked about him. "Come back," he said.

"I've got a meeting," she told him.

"Carolyn, you won't take my calls, won't talk to me, then you call up to say you've got a meeting?"

"I'll call back," she promised. "But I can't really talk now."

.   .   .

SHE FELT THAT if she had to stop her car on the freeway she'd spontaneously combust. The 405 looked paralyzed, so she drove north on Sepulveda. Sepulveda wasn't much better, but at least it gave the illusion of progress. Marty had a dinner, so she would spend the night with her son. Once she was sure Kevin was asleep, she'd call David from her cell phone.

Her gas gauge was tipping far left by the time she got to Sunset, so she kept going up to the Chevron at Moraga. The station was filled with cars, and except for an Escalade, not one of them was American. It was as if American wasn't cool. She waited for an open spot at the pump with her windows down, the late afternoon sky bright, the air warm. It was November. She said this to herself aloud. "November."

Finally a spot opened up. She was sticking the accordion nozzle into her car when somebody called her name. It was Jonathan, Marty's best friend, a tall guy who was fastidious to the point of crazy—hair always just so, shoes always shined, nothing but belts and tucked-in shirts. He drove a black Mercedes.

"I'm sorry to hear that you and Marty are having trouble," he said.

"Thank you," she said.

"If there's anything I can do," he said.

"What, Jonathan? What could you possibly do?"

He looked as if his feelings were hurt. He was forty-seven years old and had never married. He dated. He was apparently straight. He ran a real estate company. Women desperate for male company went on dates with him and refused to see him again. Those who gave him a second chance always retreated. He was the most boring man Carolyn had ever met, this guy, her husband's best friend. Sometimes, in retrospect, it shocked her how little attention she had paid to the major decisions of her life.

"I'm just saying," Jonathan said.

"Believe me, Jonathan. There is nothing you can do."

His face hardened. "What did Marty ever do to you?"

"Exactly," she said, and turned away.

Soon she was fighting her way east on Sunset. It was a good question. What had Marty ever done to her? Nothing. She'd done it to him. It was all her fault. She saw it clearly, not that it mattered. It was like a car wreck: everyone paid.

. . .

"HAVE YOU EVER thought," she asked Kevin when she got home, "about what it would be like to live somewhere else?"

"Like where?"

It had been a quiet evening—pizza for dinner, an hour and a half of TV—and now it was late and she was sitting on the side of his bed. "Move over," she told him. "Let me lie down."

She lay next to him, on top of the covers, which was how it was now. "Like somewhere other than Los Angeles," she said.

"Why would we do that?"

"I grew up somewhere else."

"Yeah."

"It wasn't so bad. You might like growing up back there, where Grandma lives."

"It's all right, but I live here. My friends are here."

"You wouldn't even consider it?" she asked.

"Mom, what is going on? Have you and Dad decided we're moving?"

"No."

"Good," he said. " 'Cause I like it here."

She wanted it to be easy, and it wasn't going to be easy. She felt exhausted just thinking about it.

"Mind if I lie here a minute?" she asked. When he was little, she would lie with him and they would fall asleep together.

"I guess, Mom, but I have a hard time falling asleep with you in the bed."

"You do?"

"You take up too much room," he said.

* * *

SHE MADE A glass of tonic water, something to soothe her stomach. She should never have asked Kevin. You didn't ask your children where they wanted to live, you told them. When had parenting become a game of deference? Kevin would adjust. Kids always did.

She finished most of her drink, topped off the glass, and called David from her cell phone. She was leaning on the kitchen counter, its granite the color of slate. He answered on the first ring.

"I don't like it that you're living with your husband," he told her.

"That's a ridiculous thing to say."

"No, it isn't. It's the truth."

"You're jealous?"

"Of course," he said. She felt a jolt, a flush in her cheeks. Jealousy was supposed to be an ugly emotion, and maybe it was, but she thought it an honest one.

"How come you've never had children?" she asked.

"I have," he answered.

A son, who'd died in a car crash. As he told the story she heard the agony in his voice. It embarrassed her, how easy her life was. How could she feel sorry for herself for being pregnant when this man had lost a child? And here she was, carrying his child.

"I'm very sorry," she said. "Why didn't you tell me?"

"Really, Carolyn? I don't like to talk about it."

She hung up and decided she would go back home. She couldn't stay in L.A., keeping up appearances, walking around divorced and pregnant with another man's child. She could be close to David. Tell him the news in person. However he reacted, she'd get through it. She'd be home, and when you had to start over, that was a good place to start.

III

MONDAY MORNING HE was watching the snow flurries dance outside his office window when he got a call from Shelly Burton. "Listen," she said. "You bought a house yet?"

"I'm renting."

"How'd you like to buy mine?" she said. She named a price. It made him consider the house. Even in Denver it would be four times what she was asking.

"That's all you want?" he asked.

"You're a hell of a negotiator."

He didn't know what to say.

"Welcome to Detroit, Mr. Halpert."

"I guess I should come out and look at it."

"Come by four," she said, "before it gets dark."

The wood and copper alone had to be worth what she was asking. More important, he liked the home, the feel of it, the stained wood that gave off an air of permanence. Still, the house was inside the city limits of Detroit, and thus in a black neighborhood. This would put off most white people; it was one of the reasons the house was so cheap, which for him made it all the better. He liked the idea of doing what others wouldn't.

. . .

HE WAS DRIVING up Livernois when his dashboard started ringing. It was Julie calling. They hadn't spoken in a couple years.

"Hey," he said.

"Hi, David. How are you?"

"I'm well. You?" They'd been married fourteen years. It always struck him as odd, because he couldn't say that he missed her, just that he missed being married. For a long time he felt it was the one thing he'd gotten right, but then, after Cory's death, it fell apart. He didn't blame her. They'd made a good run at it, but, after Cory died it didn't work anymore. Hearing her voice was still difficult.

"I'm in Denver," she said. "I know it's been a while, but I'm going to visit Cory and thought maybe you'd want to come with me."

Cory was buried in a cemetery on the west side of Denver. David had chosen the spot because it was close to the mountains. For a while he'd gone there once a week, then once a month, and then less often. He learned there was no comfort in it.

"I'm in Detroit," he said.

"Oh, too bad. You visiting your folks?"

"Actually, I moved here."

"You what? No way."

"Way," he said.

"Wow. You going to get a job back there?"

"Already got one."

"Well, I bet your parents like having you back."

"They seem to," he said.

"Wow, David. I wouldn't have guessed Detroit."

There was a long silence on the line.

"I'm sorry," he said.

"It wasn't your fault," she told him. "I know you think it was, but you're wrong."

"I'll try to believe you."

"I'm sorry I missed you. Maybe next time."

"Maybe," he allowed.

• • •

He had to admit it was a beautiful home. He'd loved the bookcase-lined living room that he remembered from his one visit. There was also a separate dining room, a large kitchen with a walk-in pantry. A wide front staircase grew right out of the large foyer. Upstairs were three bedrooms and an office. There was a guest bedroom downstairs on the main level. The master bathroom was bigger than David's office at work, with a new glass-enclosed shower but also a free-standing claw-footed tub, something out of an earlier, more prosperous era.

Cory, he thought, would have loved this place. He would have sprinted across the vast wooden floors downstairs. He would have slid down the wooden banister, then jumped two-footed into the entryway.

"It's beautiful," he told Shelly.

"You'd be the only white person on the block," she said. "Besides Mr. Belinski."

"Who's Mr. Belinski?"

"Some old white guy about two hundred years old. Fifteen years ago he killed someone breaking into his home. The shots woke Dirk up. He went there, helped him."

"Some neighborhood."

"Been no trouble since, even on Devil's Night," Shelly said.

Devil's Night was the night before Halloween. For years people had been setting houses on fire, just to watch them burn. Things were calmer now, but the whole thing shook your idea of how the world worked. It wasn't the Vandals or the Goths sacking Rome, it was as if the Romans were doing it.

His cell phone rang again. He excused himself and walked down the hallway. It was Carolyn. He knew because he'd programmed a special ring for her. "Hey there." He tried to sound happy that she was calling, which he was.

"I thought you should know I'm coming to Detroit for Thanksgiving," she said. "And I'm spending the week after."

"Great," he said. He wanted to ask whether he could see her, but he didn't.

"I'm bringing Kevin, my son. Going to my high school reunion."

"Sounds great."

"You sound weird," she said. "Where are you?"

"I'm in your brother's house."

"Why?"

"I might buy it."

"You must be out of your mind."

He admitted that she might be right.

IV

Sol GOT THE call a little after four in the afternoon. He was in bed, reading. It was one of the joys of retirement, never being needed at four in the afternoon.

"Mr. Halpert, this is Jerome Stith from Orchard Grove. I'm afraid there's been an accident."

Sol immediately knew it was serious. Usually he got calls from one of the Jamaican women. He loved the song in their voices as they gave him updates on Trudy. If it was a financial matter, he heard from a woman with the hard consonants and short vowels of his native city. Hearing from a man was a first.

"Mrs. Halpert has been taken to the hospital. She had a fall. It's quite serious."

He called David, but the kid was down in Detroit, it was rush hour, and Sol didn't want to wait at home for forty-five minutes to get picked up. And so he drove himself, once he'd brushed his hair and put on a pressed shirt and clean socks. At the hospital, he found Stith waiting outside Trudy's room, wearing a dark suit, like an undertaker. Sol's wife was unconscious, with a bruise on the left side of her face. She had a hairline fracture in her hip. The galumph had fallen on Trudy. None of the staff had actually seen it happen, and neither Trudy nor the galumph could remember the details. One of the other inmates said the galumph had tackled her.

"Tackled?" Sol asked. "What do you mean, tackled?"

"No one really knows what happened," Stith said. "All the witnesses are advanced Alzheimer cases."

Sol fumed, looked to Trudy, back to Stith, then back to Trudy again.

"Can I have some privacy?"

Sol heard Stith's retreating footfalls as he moved to the

bed. He stood looking at her until David arrived. He studied his mother and then leaned over and kissed her on the forehead. Sol realized it had never occurred to him to do that. He thanked God David was home.

"Should we sue the home?" he asked David. They were sitting by Trudy's bed, watching her sleep. A curtain separated her from the other patient. Sol spoke softly, not wanting anyone but David to hear him.

"You've got a case, perhaps, but I don't know what you'd get."

"Satisfaction?"

"I doubt that, Dad."

"What do you think happened?"

"I think he tackled her."

"Why would he do that?"

"I Googled him. He played defensive end for the Lions in the fifties. My guess is that he tackled Mom to show off for her, or just to get her approval."

"That's insane," Sol said.

"It's what men do," David said.

V

CAROLYN SAT AT one of the outside tables at the Starbucks on Beverly while around her the citizens of Beverly Hills went about their Saturday morning routines in Mercedes,

BMWs, and Lexuses. It was a little after ten, and already seventy degrees.

She had just dropped Kevin at soccer practice, after which he was going to Bobby Keane's house for the day and a sleepover. Marty was playing golf. It was wonderful to be alone, surrounded by strangers, to sit in the sun and sip a mocha and not have to be anywhere.

Still, she noticed that her pants were tight. Just that week she'd had amnio; she expected the main results by Tuesday. She'd also requested a paternity test.

"You're not sure who the father is?" the nurse asked. The woman seemed scandalized. Probably they didn't get many of these in Beverly Hills.

Carolyn was standing at the check-in counter. Now she leaned forward and spoke softly, so as not to be heard in the waiting room. "I've got a pretty good idea."

The nurse raised her eyebrows.

"But I need to be sure," Carolyn said. She handed over Marty's toothbrush. There was an outside company that did the paternity test for seven hundred bucks. They promised results Wednesday, the day before Thanksgiving. Then she'd know for sure, though she really knew already.

*   *   *

SHE NEEDED MATERNITY clothes, so she decided to walk down to a maternity shop where she'd often bought gifts for others. She moved slowly and carried her mocha, intending to buy a couple things, the first subtle outfits that would give nothing away. She didn't want to tell anyone at work. At least, not yet.

Carolyn walked into the store and there was Mandy, her therapist, buying clothes for her pregnant daughter. "Did you talk to Marty?" she asked in a whisper.

"I did." Lately, so many of Carolyn's conversations required whispers.

"And how did it go?"

"He called me despicable."

"What did you say?" Mandy asked.

"I told him I appreciated his opinion," Carolyn said. Mandy had taught her to say this. It meant *Fuck you*.

"I'll get all the details this week," Mandy said. They had an appointment Tuesday. The talk with Marty hadn't been so bad, really. Once Carolyn said she didn't want alimony, he had given in on everything else.

"You'll be fine," Mandy said. Carolyn thought Mandy might actually be right. She left the store without buying.

VI

HIS MOTHER SPENT the night in the hospital. Now David drove his father's car, the steering wheel practically bumping his chest. Sol wouldn't let him adjust the seat, said he'd never get it back to just where he liked it. David wasn't even allowed to put music on the radio, which in Detroit seemed like a crime.

"Dad, what are you going to do if Mom dies?"

"I'm going to stop going to that damn home," Sol said.

"You know what I mean."

"Son, she's already gone. Has been for some time."

They parked and walked into the hospital, David shuffling beside his father, trying to keep his pace, not rushing him. The sky hung gray and low; the air was damp and raw, and it was easy to think it portended something, but really it was always this way this time of year. Still, David sensed they were near the end with his mother—a call so early could hardly mean otherwise.

They were intercepted at the nurses' station and led to a small meeting room off a larger waiting area. The nurse offered them coffee. "Let me get the doctor," she said.

His complexion was dark, this doctor, his eyes baggy and hooded, a veneer of stubble above them that covered his head. "I'm Dr. Czerny," he said. "I'm very sorry, but Mrs. Halpert has died."

"Of what?" Sol wanted to know.

"Her injuries. I was paged around two this morning. The nurses noticed she was developing problems with her respiration and blood pressure. It would seem she had a ruptured spleen."

"You couldn't figure this out yesterday when they brought her in?" David asked. It was, he knew, the question to ask, but what did it matter now?

The doctor started to speak but stopped, and then

David became aware of his father. They were all sitting around a table of fake wood, the kind of thing you'd find in a breakfast nook. The walls were plain, the color of paste. His father's shoulders were jerking, almost heaving. And then they heaved. "Oh God," Sol said, and the tears came. David gave a quick glimpse at the doctor and then pushed his chair back, knelt by his father. He put an arm around his father's back. "It's all right, Dad," he said. "It's over."

With each gasp his father seemed to let go a small store of reserve, till he was crying as David had never seen him cry, as David had never cried, except perhaps the night of Cory's death.

*   *   *

THAT NIGHT HE slept in his old room. He didn't think his father should be alone. It was a fitful night. He woke often, disoriented, middle-aged but back in the room of his teenage years, in his old bed. He looked through the darkness to the same bookshelf he'd seen every morning as he was growing up. It created a kind of vertigo.

The following afternoon he called the nursing home to tell them his mother wouldn't be coming back and made arrangements to get her things. He spoke to Arlene, one of the Jamaican women. It had been an awful day, but Arlene's voice lifted his mood. "Oh, I am so sorry," she said. "And poor Mr. Jovanovich."

"He notices she's gone?"

"Oh, yes. All day he looks for her."

David thought that his mother might have enjoyed life more if she could have known that when she was gone there would be two men crying for her. He vowed to try to live as if he'd be missed.

. . .

IT WAS ALMOST two in the morning when he called Carolyn. She took the call, said she was driving home from a night out with friends. Immediately he felt jealous, but he kept it to himself.

"My mother died today," he told her.

"Oh, David. I'm very sorry."

"Thanks."

"I ended it with Marty yesterday. It's all over but the crying."

"Who's going to cry?"

"My son," she said.

He didn't have an answer. She asked when the funeral was, then told him that she'd be there.

"You don't have to do that."

"I know," she said. "Now, what's this about you buying my brother's house?"

. . .

SHE FLEW IN the next day, would go to the funeral the following morning and back to L.A. that night so she could pick up her son and bring him right back to Detroit. It was difficult and inconvenient for her, and he was moved by it.

His father's cousin, Milt Jones, also came to town. Milt drove David's father to the funeral so David could pick up Carolyn. It had been some weeks since he'd seen her, and for a moment, waiting at the door of her mother's town-home, he worried that she would seem a stranger. Then she opened the door, beautiful as ever, and he realized how silly he was. She sat in his car and it felt to him as if she'd never left.

"Stop saying that," she told him. They were pulling away and he'd again thanked her for coming. "I wanted to come."

Again he had to stop himself from saying thank you.

"It's been a tough year for us," she said. "I thought you could use a friend."

"I can," he admitted. A long silence followed. There was so much he wanted to say to her, but his mother was dead and what he was feeling was too complicated for words.

"It's okay," she told him, as if reading his mind. "Just drive. We'll talk later."

They drove straight to the funeral. The radio played music that had been new when he was young but was now called classic: Mitch Ryder, Bob Seger, Glenn Frey, Ted Nugent, Alice Cooper. Detroiters all. It was difficult for David to explain the pride he felt in his city, but certainly this music was behind it. Throw in John Lee Hooker and Aretha Franklin and Marvin Gaye, Stevie Wonder, Diana Ross, Smokey Robinson and the rest of Motown, the jazz of

Carter, Burrell, and Henderson, the power of the MC5 and the Stooges, the pop of Madonna, and the current efforts of Ritchie, Mathers, and White, and you could argue that what the Motor City really made, the thing that would last long after the Ren Cen crumbled into the river and the world no longer needed cars, was music.

*   *   *

THE TREES THREW long shadows across the cemetery lawn, which in November was a faded army green. The rabbi had brought several men from the temple to be sure to fill out the minyan. David stood with his father and cousin Milt, all of them close to the grave. With the rabbi and the extra men they totaled seven; ten were needed to say the mourners' prayer. When it came to the dead, Jews wanted witnesses, but this was Detroit and witnesses were hard to find. Steve Bergen was there, and two of Trudy's friends, each with a daughter in tow, and Carolyn, but there wasn't a bar or bat mitzvah among them. David watched as the rabbi said a few words to Sol and made a call on his cell phone. Twenty minutes later a car arrived with three fifteen-year-old boys from the confirmation class, dressed in baggy pants and hooded sweatshirts, like black kids from the Cass corridor.

They began the Kaddish, the prayer for the dead. David mumbled the words, unsure if he really still knew them but aware that his recitation was one of the ten that counted.

. . .

AFTER THE FUNERAL, he drove Carolyn back to her mother's. Tomorrow she was flying back to California to retrieve her son. She had traveled all that way for him.

"Tell me I'll see you when you come back," he said. He couldn't help himself. He missed her already.

"You will," she promised.

He felt an inkling of calm, just knowing he'd see her again. He leaned across the seat and gave her a kiss, a chaste one, as befit the occasion.

VII

CAROLYN CALLED HER mother from the gate when it was clear the plane would be on time. Kevin sat beside her reading a book he'd been assigned for the break. It had a dragon on the cover. Around them in the industrial light of the airport, people sat reading, staring at laptops, listening to music with earphones, talking into cell phones.

"You know what I heard today?" her mother said. "Your friend David is buying Shelly's house."

"He told me."

"Shelly is very excited to be able to move away."

"I'm sure she'll be happy," Carolyn said. Someone was ringing in. She put her mother on hold.

"I'm trying to reach Carolyn Evans," said a female voice.

"This is she."

"I'm calling from Genetic Services regarding the paternity test you ordered."

"Yes?" She felt her heart beating in her chest.

"Paternity was not confirmed."

"Not confirmed?"

"Yes," said the woman. "The man whose genetic material you provided is not the father of the child."

So it was David.

"Thank you," Carolyn said. She clicked back to her mother. "Mom, are you still there?"

"Yes. I've got your rooms all ready," her mother responded.

"Great, Mom, but look, I've got to go. They're calling our plane." She hung up.

"They are?" asked Kevin.

"No, I lied to get off the phone with Grandma," she told him. He looked straight ahead as he considered this and then went back to his book, lesson learned. Probably he would tell little fibs to her the rest of her life, and she'd deserve it.

• • •

LATE ON HER first night back she met David at the site of their first date. She'd known she'd been carrying his child, and now she had scientific proof. It made her think of him ever more fondly. She had to find a way to tell him.

"You're out of your mind," she said. They were talking about Dirk's house.

"You know, there are luxury cars that cost more than that house."

"Note to David: you're white." The bartender came by, and she ordered a tonic water.

"Don't you want something stronger?"

"I want to know why you'd move into a black neighborhood."

"I love that house, and I want to live in the city. All my life I've told people I'm from Detroit. I want to really mean it. I'm back. All in."

All in? She didn't know what to say to that.

"Why don't you come over to my place?" he said.

"Whoa, a booty call."

"What have you got to lose?" he said.

Nothing, she decided, but sex had solved nothing for her.

"I'm not coming over."

"You look beautiful."

"I'm still not coming over," she said.

She waited for him to sip his drink and then look back at her. "You know," she said, "there was a time when Natalie thought she was pregnant. With your child."

"She never told me."

"She didn't want you to freak out."

"What's that supposed to mean?"

"She thought you'd lose it."

"I was seventeen. I would have lost it," he admitted.

"And so you had a child with someone else," she said.

It sounded like an accusation, though she hadn't meant it that way. The bartender, she noticed, moved away. He was a young guy with sideburns right out of the sixties. He started to load glasses into his little dishwasher, making more noise than could possibly have been necessary.

David got more handsome the longer she looked at him. "What?" he asked.

"What, what?"

"What do you want from me?"

She intended not to answer, to say nothing at all, but then the truth came out, as it sometimes did. "A little time," she said.

VIII

HIS FATHER HAD made a reservation at the Holiday Inn because they had room and the price was reasonable and there were just two of them and who cooks Thanksgiving dinner for two people? Still, David couldn't help but tease him. "The Holiday Inn, Dad? Why not Chinese take-out?"

"Don't be a putz," his father told him. "It's Thanksgiving."

David drove. It was late—not in the day, but relative to the reservation—and his father wanted him to hurry. "They're not going to give the table away. We'll be the only ones there," David insisted.

He was wrong. The lobby was packed, with many of

those there speaking something other than English. Span-
ish, Polish or Russian, something else he couldn't place.
It made sense, now that David thought about it. If you
were born in Hungary, say, what would you know of the
Thanksgiving meal? Of course, there were also plenty of
American-born patrons, white and black. David made his
way to the hostess stand and gave his name.

"Dad, would you look at this?" he said. "Lots of other
people who don't want to cook Thanksgiving dinner either."

The hostess led them out of the dining room to the
enclosed pool area, which was set up with tables and where
there were already fifty people or so enjoying the holiday
meal. His father asked for something inside.

"We're all filled up," said the hostess.

"Go with it, Dad," said David. "Out here you get the
full experience."

They sat. Above the din—or perhaps under it—David
could hear the workings of the pool machinery. "That smell.
That chlorine smell. I guess now it means Thanksgiving."

"I didn't know about the pool," his father said.

"It's okay," David said.

"It's the first Thanksgiving without Mom," his father
said.

David nodded.

"Your problem," his father said, "is that you're too
unencumbered."

"Too unencumbered?"

"Yes. You lack the basic chattel of life—a wife, children, debt. These things give a man purpose."

Maybe, David thought, though he had had all that chattel, and look where it had got him.

His father talked on. "Most men, they get up in the morning, they go off to work, and they know why: they've got a family to feed. It's been that way forever. It drives the world. The animal world, too. You, you get up in the morning and then—why do you go off to work?"

"To make you happy," David said.

"Make me happy?" his father asked.

"Sure, so when someone says to you, 'How's David doing?' you don't have to answer, 'He's home on the couch drinking vodka from the bottle.' "

"You're mocking me," his father said.

"Maybe, Dad, but just a little."

"I'm trying to help you. This is what's so lousy about getting old: I finally know what to do, and I'm too old to do it."

"You're arguing for chattel," David said.

"How 'bout just a woman?" his father asked. "Someone who makes you happy. It's no good for a man to be alone."

"You're alone, Dad."

"I'm not alone," he said.

David looked at him, worried suddenly that now his father, too, was losing his mind.

"I'm not alone," his father explained, "because you're back."

IX

THE NIGHT OF Thanksgiving she lay beside him and listened to him breathe. She'd promised herself that she wouldn't do this, that she would put everything on the table first, but then she'd gone ahead and broken that promise. David was asleep already, and she was still damp from making love. She pulled the sheet up, and then the covers, a duvet really too small for two people.

She allowed herself to doze for half an hour, and then she slid out of bed and left him sleeping. She considered him in the shadows, flat on his back, eyes covered, elbow draped over the bridge of his nose. She once read that how a man slept told you a lot about him. There was one type you were supposed to avoid, but she didn't think it was the back sleepers. No, it was the guys who slept diagonally. She'd known a couple.

David, she thought, carried his sadness with him. You could watch him sleep and know he was a decent man.

On the drive back to her mother's, she decided she needed to tell David now she was pregnant with his child. It was getting so that dreading it was perhaps worse than actually going through with it. Also, she needed to tell Kevin they were moving. Then she'd take him back to L.A. to finish the semester and say goodbye to his friends. And to his father.

X

FRIDAY MORNING HE watched the football highlights on ESPN. The Lions had lost again. He tried to remember the last time Detroit had won on Thanksgiving Day. He'd probably been living in Denver and hadn't noticed.

The Thanksgiving meal had been a disaster, but it had been a short disaster, and for that David was thankful. Family obligations were usually horrible, unless you didn't have them at all.

He hoped Carolyn would come by again tonight. He was happy when she was with him; it was that simple. He took pleasure in the double-take she sometimes gave him, or how she would sit on the couch, legs up, her feet pushing against his thigh while he sat at the other end. It was rare what they had, he thought. He knew things usually got complicated. He told himself not to fear what he wouldn't have in the future, just to focus on what he had now.

His cell phone rang. He answered without looking. At this time it could only be her.

"Hey," he said.

"Yo, you David Halpert?"

"Yes. Who's this?"

"Eric McCall."

David reached for the remote and hit the mute button. It was Marlon's friend. David had gotten his number from Michelle in a last-ditch effort to find Marlon. David had left a message to call back on his cell number, worrying that the law firm's receptionists might scare the kid off. "Thanks for calling back," David said.

"Yeah, you leave a message like that, you get a call back, you know?"

"So, do you have a number for Marlon?"

"I got Marlon. He right here. Wants to know if you're for real. Whose money you giving?"

"It's an inheritance from Dirk Burton."

The phone went silent, and then a new voice came on.

"This Marlon Booker."

"You're a hard man to find, Marlon."

"Not if you know where to look."

He asked Marlon his date of birth, his mother's name. He was the right Marlon Booker. Marlon agreed to come to David's office, but he wanted cash. *Cash?* Unbelievable.

"I can't give you cash," David said.

"Why can't you?"

"First, because I need a record of the disbursement for the estate and for the government. Second, because a hundred thou cash takes up a lot of space. What, you want a sack with a dollar sign on it?"

"Maybe no dollar sign."

"You've got to take a check. Come to my office."

"Be there in a couple hours. Where's it at? Out in 248?"

"I'm not working today. It's the Friday after Thanksgiving." A thought occurred to David. "I guess you've got something to be thankful for. Did you go out to Ypsilanti to be with your mother?"

"It's Thanksgiving?" Marlon said.

• • •

David's mother was dead, and he'd spent enough time with his father. The woman he loved was AWOL. Later there would be a college game on the tube, some Big 12 matchup, which he still thought of as obscure, though he had lived for years in a Big 12 state. His idea for the day was to put his financial affairs in order, in preparation for the house purchase: balance the checkbook, file the brokerage statements, make sure everything was ready to go. This took twenty-five minutes. The house was so cheap he was paying cash.

He decided to take a drive down to see the house. Shelly was in Texas. He wished he could get in and walk around, lay out how he would live there, but he was happy just to check out the neighborhood.

November, Michigan style: gray sky hovering atop the telephone poles, brown leaves, faded grass, snow flurries swirling, as though circling down a drain. On Shelly's street—his new street—dead leaves collected along curbs, along with the occasional American-made car. A few black kids—eleven years old, twelve, a couple with green Michigan State ski hats—were playing touch football, one of them hamming it up, the other yelling, "I got you! I got you!" The ham shook his head. "Nuh-huh," he answered.

He thought about Cory. He could feel it, as though the boy were here. He'd be older now, sixteen. It was Thanksgiving. You were supposed to be with your children on Thanksgiving: it was the natural order of things.

David remembered a time when Cory was eleven. He had a friend named Andy Cash, who lived in a four-thousand-square-foot house two blocks away and always seemed to be starving. David made Cory's school lunches, and one day Cory said, "I need two sandwiches."

"Why?"

"I get hungry."

He was a thin kid, and there was no way he was eating two sandwiches, but David made them. Soon Cory was asking for extra chips, a second apple.

David remembered the day. It was snowing, the air full of the big, wet flakes of late April in Denver, while the week before it had almost reached eighty degrees.

"Sit down," David told him. He joined his son at the kitchen table. "I know you're not eating two sandwiches or two apples. I also know it's not right to lie, especially to your own father. So just tell me, what are you doing with the food?"

The boy looked stricken, caught. "You won't get mad?"

"I doubt it," David said.

"It's Andy, Dad. He's got nothing."

"What do you mean, nothing?" Andy's father was some big-shot lawyer for Qwest.

"No lunch. He never has any lunch."

"Can't he buy?"

"His parents, they never give him any money for lunch. They forget, I guess."

"Who gets up with him, gets him off to school?"

"No one. He does that himself."

Eleven years old. David felt his heart tear a little for his son, who would steal food for a friend. You can try to teach your kids to be generous, he thought, but really they either have it in them or they don't.

"Tell you what," he told Cory. "From now on, I'll make lunch for Andy. And you don't hide things from me. Deal?"

"Deal." Cory smiled, and David thought, *This is what it's all about.*

* * *

Now HE SAT in the car and watched a few more plays, and then he got out of the car, surprised to find a man standing on the sidewalk, waiting for him.

He was a stocky guy in an overcoat, hands thrust deep in his pockets. "May I help you?" he asked.

"I'm David Halpert. I'm buying this house."

The man looked at Shelly's house, then back at David.

"Shelly's?" the man said.

"Yeah. Great place. Thought I'd come over, take another look."

"Where you from?" asked the man.

"Most recently Denver, but I grew up in Detroit."

"Detroit?"

"Birmingham," David admitted.

"So you've got some idea what you're doing."

"Being the white guy, you mean."

The man smiled. "I'm Russell Wilson," he said. "I live next door." He pointed behind him, then looked at his place, as if to make sure it was still there. "Listen, you want to come over, have a cup of coffee?"

Wilson's house was at least as big as Shelly's, though slightly different in style. "Craftsman" was the word that came to David's mind, though he was no expert in architecture or design. Around the house were pictures of children who would now be grown and of what David took to be grandchildren. David ended up in the kitchen, where he met Susan Wilson, a trim woman, formally dressed.

"Really?" she said when she heard David would soon be a neighbor. She went to work on the coffee.

Wilson had been a judge but was now one year into retirement. He'd bought the house in the summer of '68, "when I was a young man." What he left unspoken was that it had been the year after the riots. Fires had burned whole blocks as tanks rolled down the streets of Detroit. By the next year, whites were giving their homes away and moving out of the city.

Wilson grilled David on his life, especially why he was moving here. "You understand, you'll be the only white person," Wilson said more than once, as if he feared maybe David didn't understand. And so David kept saying the truth, which was that he did indeed know what Wilson was saying. It was hard to make people understand that he was committed to the idea of return, that he was coming home, all the way, and he wasn't going to be dissuaded by the racial striation of his city or the expectations of its citizens. He was, for once, doing things his own way. He was forty-five years old; this would be the last great adventure of his life.

Wilson was impressed that David had known Dirk Burton. "Quite a man," Wilson said. He sipped his coffee and put the cup back on its saucer in a way that David thought was making some sort of point about Dirk, or maybe race, or maybe both. At this point it seemed better not to ask for clarification.

"So tell me," Wilson finally said. "Are you the white Moses? Is there now going to be a steady stream of white folk making their way back to Palmer Woods after wandering forty years in the suburban wilderness, or . . ." Here he paused for words, or maybe just breath. "Or, David Halpert, are you just the one lunatic who wants to come back?"

"I'm the one lunatic," David admitted.

XI

E-CALL WANTED TO go with him, said there was no other way. He'd wear his 9mm in his waistband with the big hoodie. You get a call that's too good to be true—*one hundred G's*—then it's too good to be true. If this guy David was for real, no one would see anything. But E-Call smelled a rat.

"No, Dirk, he was like an uncle, he told me he was leaving me money," Marlon explained. He had thought it would be a decent number, like five grand. A hundred grand? It was crazy; it did *seem* like a setup. If Elvis was behind it, then he knew that E-Call was hiding Marlon and they'd go to this meeting and end up dead or have to shoot their way out, which he'd never done. It was times like this he asked himself how he'd gotten into this life, but the answer was simple enough: he'd followed E-Call. His brother. Marlon had always liked to go where he knew someone, and this was no different.

" 'Kay," Marlon said. "You bring the gun. I'll drive."

"You're gonna go meet some white man in a suit in that piece-a-shit car?" E-Call said. True enough, but there was no stress in owning a beater. It was something Marlon had learned from his father.

"I think we missed Thanksgiving," Marlon said.

"It's next Thursday, right?"

"Yesterday." They'd spent it inside, playing video games. Marlon didn't go out much, because there was no way to know who he might run into. He wondered now what his mother had done for the holiday. In any case, he couldn't visit her; he wanted to stay low till the coast was clear. The woman had enough trouble without her son bringing more home.

"You think we'll know each other in forty years?" Marlon asked. He tried to imagine his friend as an old man, but the only thing he could come up with was an image of gray hair. People, he knew, aged in different ways than that.

"Shit, I'm behind a week as it is."

"Just thinking ahead."

"Just like I used to tell everyone about you. 'He's more than just quiet,' I'd say. 'Wheels are turning.'" E-Call paused. "If it's real, this lawyer thing, what you gonna do with all that money? You could actually buy a Benz with that much."

"And then what if Elvis sees me?"

"Shit, man," E-Call said, almost mesmerized in thought. "You buy that Benz and you drive the hell away."

XII

SHE'D BEEN TO her tenth reunion, which had been held at the Pontiac Silverdome, that stadium with the inflated roof that wasn't any better for reunions than it had been for football games or rock concerts. Some architect had designed the building, she thought. It was the product of human design, unfettered by the messiness of love and family, and still it was shit. Soulless and depressing. Now she was at a banquet hall in Pontiac, the southern end of Pontiac, but still Pontiac. From the looks of it, maybe the same architect.

She had to park far from the door and then walk along the line of cars, most of them American, illuminated by the buzzing street lamps. It was freezing, the air of her youth. She finally reached the hall, the automatic doors opened, and she stepped in from the cold.

"Carolyn!"

She looked up and there was a girl she knew she should know, they had hung together all through sophomore year, stayed friends till Carolyn left town after high school, which was the last time they talked.

"Oh my God, you look exactly the same. I mean, exactly. How do you do it?"

"I don't know," Carolyn said. Tracy, Theresa, Terry. Something with a T, she thought.

They went to the coat check, Carolyn feeling a little shy. Who else was going to come up to her whose name she wouldn't be able to remember? This was the Midwest, and they would all be well-meaning. She was beginning to hate the whole idea of well-meaning, because well-meaning required a response.

There was a guy at the coat check and Carolyn couldn't help but notice him. He was tall, lean, had a full head of dark hair and dark, kind eyes, eyes not unlike David's, which were, she thought, David's best feature. They showed his basic intelligence and depth. Like David, this man was handsome, able to attract attention when he walked into a room. He took his claim check and headed back toward the hall.

"Who was that?"

"Never seen him before," Carolyn said.

The next step, thank God, was the name-tag table. Theresa it was. "Let's get a drink," she said.

Carolyn followed Theresa into the hall, packed already with a couple hundred people, a room full of strangers with a full bar, which, Carolyn had to admit, was her kind of party. An Irish whisky would have been lovely.

It was about an hour later when Suzy found her. Carolyn was nursing her second tonic water while looking at a board from homecoming senior year. Carolyn had been lesser royalty in that homecoming court, and there was a picture of all of them standing on a float parked at the fifty-yard line at halftime, all smiles, though Carolyn remembered that the night had been as cold as this one, and that she'd been embarrassed to stand next to Monica Honans, who was so beautiful, and apparently not at the reunion.

"How are you?" Suzy asked.

"I ended my marriage," Carolyn said. "You were right."

In the background the band started up "Sweet Home, Alabama."

"I'm sorry," said Suzy.

"Well," Carolyn said, "I'm less miserable."

The handsome man from the coat check walked by. Carolyn and Suzy watched him pass.

"Look at Paul Michalowski, all grown up."

"Who is he?" Carolyn asked.

"Exactly. Never even noticed him in high school, and now look."

"What's he do?"

"He's a bankruptcy attorney. Not for people but for corporations."

"Looks like he's doing well."

"Yeah, well, business is booming."

• • •

Ten minutes later, Carolyn found herself standing close to him. "Excuse me," he said, "but aren't you Carolyn Evans?"

"I am."

He smiled down at her. It was almost paternalistic, that smile. "Paul Michalowski. I asked you out once, to homecoming dance, tenth grade. You said no."

"I was a bitch then," she said. "I mean, what did I know?"

He chuckled. "What did any of us know?"

• • •

She ran out to her car, the air biting. Her eyes teared. She turned the engine over, then ran back to the vestibule to wait. It reminded her of being a girl, when her father would let her start the car in winter. How old was she then? Fourteen, maybe. Now her classmates were trickling out, though the band was still playing, this time an endless version of "Sympathy for the Devil." Dale Mortola came up to her.

She'd looked for him. She'd lost her virginity to him, the typical fiasco; the whole experience should have been enough to put her off sex for good, though of course it hadn't. "It'll get better," Natalie had assured her at the time. Now she realized that Natalie had been talking about David. And she was right.

"I was hoping you'd be here," Dale said. "And I'm surprised you are. Thought you'd be a million miles away."

"Me, too."

"I'm sorry about Natalie. I mean, it's horrible."

"Yes, it is."

He asked questions and she answered, aware that she should ask him about himself. Deep down he was a sweet guy, kind, caring, from the look of him not all that successful. His wife came up, a plump woman with an elaborate hairdo, hair stacked on her head with tendrils dropping down, the whole effect unfortunate. But then she moved to him, put her arm around his waist, and he returned the gesture and smiled, and Carolyn thought, *Look at that, these two people are still in love.*

She drove home feeling that she was getting it down, the cold and heating cars and the old boyfriends, the whole world she'd lost still there, beating away, if a bit more decrepit. It was snowing fairly hard now. The wipers swept the white flakes away from her windshield in a rhythm that made it seem there was a dream or a memory out there, if she looked hard enough into the darkness.

XIII

SONOFABITCH IF THERE weren't two or three inches of snow in the yard, on the driveway, and it was still Thanksgiving weekend. Sol, as a young man, had always welcomed the snow, the clean freshness of it——even on those brutally cold nights in Korea he had appreciated the snow—but lately he was beginning to see it for the pain in the ass others thought it was. Now, for instance, he wanted the paper and it was at the end of his white driveway. He kicked around in the closet, trying to find his boots, and then decided he'd just wear his loafers. It was only to the end of the drive and back—why make a federal case out of a minute or two of cold feet?

And cold they were—he didn't bother with socks either—as he made his way down the drive. It was slippery, and with each step he could feel a little sliding. He slowed, careful not to fall. Down at the street was the *Free Press*, wrapped in a plastic cover, along with the part of the Sunday paper that could be delivered on Saturday. Once he'd sent David to do this. He bent and grabbed the freezing plastic bag. As he stood a car honked its horn, and when he turned to look he lost his footing. He never saw the car, just heard it retreating. Maybe it was two cars. His hip was on fire with pain, though he was lying in the snow. *Christ,* he thought. *A broken hip, maybe.*

Or maybe not. He lay there on the cold pavement, afraid to move. It was his right hip. Also his right hand and wrist. He moved the hand slightly, then his body, to get flat on his back. It was freezing. Above, the sky was gray, a deep whitish gray that seemed very close, or possibly very far away.

The thought occurred to him, clearly and calmly, that he might die, that the end could come in just such a ridiculous way. He thought of his wife, tackled to death. Wasn't the moment of death always unexpected in that way?

"Hey, mister, let me help you up."

He heard this and was at first unsure if he was dreaming it, but there was a kid there, blue eyes, head of blond stubble. "You okay?" the kid said.

"I fell." Sol reached out a hand. "Help me sit up."

The kid did as instructed. Sol sat. His hip hurt, but it wasn't too bad. He looked at the kid. "Who are you?"

"Brian Kleinstadt, from down the block. You need me to call an ambulance?"

Sol noticed his decrepit car parked along the curb, an old Camaro skirted in rust. "Not yet. Let's see if I can stand."

The kid walked him to the house, even carried the paper. He helped Sol to his couch. Sol felt embarrassed by the mess of the room and by his weakness, especially when he was maneuvered by this specimen of Aryan physicality. It wasn't what he would have expected, though. The kid had done a mitzvah.

"You sure you're going to be okay?" the kid asked.

"I'm good," Sol said. It was what young people said nowadays, apparently without irony. "Will you excuse me if I don't see you out? I'm very grateful, though."

Once the kid left, he called Cathy Brown. He could have called David, but he'd asked enough of his son. Cathy Brown was a shiksa he saw from time to time, the perfect woman because she always waited to be called. He asked her to come over and make him tea. He had a chill. "Actually, I can't," he said when she suggested he make it himself. He wouldn't say more.

He knew she would hurry over. He also knew he would be fine, for now, but that in time he might look back on this day as the beginning of the end.

XIV

MARLON SHOWED ALMOST an hour late, but David didn't mind. He had plenty of work now. He'd found that Detroiters were far more amenable to planning for their deaths than the people of Denver, and whether it was Michigan's economy, its lack of consistent sunlight, or something deeper in the midwestern soul, to David this made a certain intuitive sense.

He walked out to the lobby to get Marlon. Heather, the front receptionist, a pretty girl still in her twenties, no doubt planning her escape to Atlanta or San Diego, made eyes at David. What-the-fuck eyes. There were two young black men. One slouched in his chair, one of those kids gaunt in a way that seemed almost feline, though he wore clothes big enough for a 250-pound man, also a baseball cap with a Detroit Tiger Olde English *D,* and earphones around his neck. He looked like a guy who worked on an airport tarmac. Next to him the other kid was similarly dressed, this one with narrow, almost Tartar eyes and earphones emitting a scratchy beat.

Neither looked at David. Maybe enough suits had already walked by that they didn't feel the need to look up.

"I'm David Halpert," David said.

The kid with the Tigers cap snapped to attention. This what a hundred grand could do.

"I'm Marlon," he said. "Booker."

They shook hands. The other kid removed his earphones. "This is E-Call," Marlon said. "Eric McCall."

McCall nodded but didn't offer his hand.

"Well, Marlon, we should go to my office," David said. "If Mr. McCall would like to—"

"You good?" McCall asked Marlon, and got a nod. McCall looked around, and David realized he didn't know what to do.

"You can wait here," David said. "Would you like something to drink?"

"Huh?" the kid said.

"A drink? A Coke, maybe? We've got Vernor's. Something while you wait."

A moment passed. "Coke, then," David suggested.

"What's it cost?" the kid asked.

"No, no, Mr. McCall. We're happy to give you the Coke."

McCall looked at Marlon, who shrugged and said, "I'll take a Vernor's."

"Me, too," said McCall.

David nodded to Heather, and she headed off, reluctantly.

David and Marlon walked back to David's office, Marlon

looking around as if he expected to be followed. David had to practically force him to sit in a chair. Heather appeared with his drink.

"Okay, Marlon," he said. "I need some ID, like a driver's license, and your signature, and I'll get a check out."

"Sure would like cash if you could do it," Marlon said.

"I can't. You know, the tax is taken care of."

"Tax?" the kid said.

"You won't owe tax."

"Okay."

"So why worry about cash?"

Marlon leaned forward, spoke softly. "Who am I gonna get to cash that sucker?"

"A bank. Don't you have a bank account?"

Marlon sat back as if to say, *No, of course not.*

"Get a bank account. Deposit the money. Then save it. Do you have anyone who advises you on financial matters?" It sounded crazy to say this as soon as it came out of his mouth. This kid wore a Tigers cap indoors, sideways on his head.

"Advise me?" Marlon said.

XV

E-CALL OFFERED TO come this time, too, but Marlon didn't want him. Even E-Call admitted that this David guy wasn't dangerous and probably didn't want Marlon's money. Or if he did, he was going to take it with a briefcase, not a gun, and E-Call wasn't going to be any help at all. The real issue was that Marlon needed David to like him. David would soon be living in Dirk's house; Shelly was already gone. Marlon had to get back in there and get his money; it would be best to be invited.

They were meeting at a bank. Marlon never went to banks—"Nothing but security cameras," E-Call warned—but Marlon figured that this might be the way to go. Put some money where no one could get at it, not even the police, because it was legal cash. It was an idea that always gave Marlon pause: all that money, legal.

The bank was Comerica, same name as where they played baseball now. Marlon needed an address, and so he used his mom's in Ypsilanti, same as his driver's license. He signed the back of the check, above the line, as instructed, and they gave him a receipt for the money, a one and five zeros. Then the dot and two more zeros. He got a booklet with checks. He'd have to find out how to use them. He got a cash card to let him get at the money, up to three hundred bucks at a time. He set a secret number—he used E-Call's birthday—and David showed him how to use the card.

Back on the street, Marlon needed clarification. "So, you write out the number here?"

"That's right, then put the number of cents over one hundred."

"I seen that," Marlon said, though he never knew why it was that way. He liked having this one mystery solved.

"You didn't have to do that, right?" he said to David. "Take me in there."

"No," David said.

"So why you do it?"

"Someone had to."

"You one a those do-gooders? Good Christian and all that?"

"Not even close, Marlon."

"You expecting a tip?"

David laughed, a real laugh, and Marlon felt embarrassed because he didn't understand what was funny. The man didn't want money, and there obviously was no woman involved, and so it was hard to know what he was up to. Maybe he really was one of those always-guilty, churchgoing types who wanted to help his fellow man.

"No tip," David said.

"Michelle says you're buying Shelly's house."

"That's right."

"You crazy, huh?" The man seemed to know a lot about the larger world—wills and banks and cash cards and such—but nothing about the place he was standing in at any particular moment. He didn't even notice that he was moving into a neighborhood where white people didn't live.

"Certifiable," David said. He looked back at the bank. "You know," he said, as if he knew what Marlon was thinking, "with all that money in the bank, you could change your life."

"You really think that happens?"

"I do, all the time," said David. "Just look at me."

"What's changed about you?"

"Everything."

"You're still a lawyer," Marlon said.

"I'm saying that you can do better, Marlon. You can change—and you have the chance to do so. You can be somebody."

Marlon appreciated that David expected more of him. No one else really ever expected anything. "Why you care?"

David stood there a moment, seriously thinking on the question.

"I don't know," he said. "I just do."

XVI

Carolyn walked into the kitchen to find Tina making a cup of tea. It was time to face up to things.

"Want one?" her mother asked.

"Mom, I'm pregnant. Also, Marty and I are splitting up."

Her mother turned and looked at her as if she were a stranger, someone who'd just come in off the street.

"It's not Marty's," she added.

Her mother walked over to the table and sat down.

"And I'm moving," Carolyn said. "Back here."

"To Detroit?"

"Yes."

"But what about Kevin?"

"He's coming with me."

Tina slowly shook her head and looked out the window. It was three in the afternoon, the light outside fighting its way around a pine tree.

"Everything is falling apart," her mother said.

"You'll have another grandchild," Carolyn said.

"Sit," her mother said.

Carolyn sat. Her mother reached out and took her hand.

"Whose child are you carrying?"

"I'd rather not say yet. I mean, until I tell him."

"You are in trouble. That's why you're coming home."

"Something like that, Mom."

"What does Kevin say?"

"He doesn't know yet."

"You must tell him."

"Of course."

"He might forgive you someday," her mother said. "If you're lucky."

· · ·

THERE WAS NO choice now but to act deliberately, with forethought. Most people considered options a good thing, the American way, but one tended to squander those choices, or to choose badly, and then to call a bad outcome fate, as if the choices made had nothing to do with it.

Carolyn had grown up with all the advantages and now she felt she needed to give them to Kevin, and to her new child. This seemed easier in Detroit, with its lesser stores of social pressure and conspicuous consumption; with its unsettled weather; with its lowered expectations of how well things might turn out. Oddly, she thought this didn't inhibit ambition but aided it: in California you might believe things came easily, while here you learned you had to work hard. She really couldn't think of a better place to raise kids.

And then there was David. She realized she was afraid to tell him about the child because she thought she might lose him. She cared for him; she was willing to admit this to herself. In fact, she loved him. It scared her how precarious the outcome seemed. Once she told him about the baby, he'd make a decision, and what if he decided differently than she hoped? It exhausted her just to think about it. But she had to tell him. And soon.

·   ·   ·

KEVIN CRIED. At first there were just tears, and then when he realized his mother's mind could not be changed, he wailed. She tried to comfort him, but he pulled away and then ran from the room. He locked himself in his bedroom. Carolyn insisted he open the door, pounded on it, put her shoulder to the wood, but he was on the other side, braced against it. He was twelve now, and stronger than she was.

"Open this door!" she shouted. "Or you're grounded."

"I don't care!" he shouted back. "You've already grounded me for my life."

She left him there and went outside. It was quarter to

six in the evening, completely dark and freezing. She drew deep breaths of air, felt that odd coolness inside her, almost like water going down. She told herself she was doing the right thing. Then she said it again, aloud, so that it would be easier to believe.

XVII

THE POUNDING ON the door made him freeze. He'd been in the house a little over four hours, since right after the closing. He felt his heart racing, his mind slowly conjuring up the word: fear. Who was pounding on the door? "It's okay," he told himself. He said this aloud. The words, the sound of them, made him feel a little less alone. Besides, thieves didn't knock.

He'd been in the kitchen, looking in the cupboards— he'd bought not only the house but most of its contents— and now he walked to the door and opened it. There was Marlon in a puffy down jacket, his breath a cloud of smoke around his head. It was half past six, as dark as the middle of any night.

"Hey, can I come in, Mr. Halpert? Damn cold out."

David took him to the living room, flipped on the light.

"Nothing's changed," Marlon said. "Even the books and shit."

"You a reader, Marlon?"

"Nah, not me. The paper, once in a while. Follow some basketball, but you can get everything you need from the TV, ESPN, you know?"

"Take your coat off, sit down," David said. "You want something?"

"You mean like a Vernor's?"

"I don't know if I have any. I just moved in, but Shelly left everything. I bet I can find something."

"Dirk, he liked gin. Bet there's a bottle. You like a martini?"

"Sure," David said, amused at Marlon trying to play the host.

"Mind if I make a couple?" Marlon asked.

"Mind if I ask you a question first?" David said, thinking there was no way this kid came over to tend bar.

"What?"

"What are you doing here?"

"Let me make the martinis, and I'll get right down to it."

David wasn't sure what he should say. Barging into someone's house and making drinks with his liquor was no one's idea of polite society, though Marlon obviously thought about it differently.

"What is it, Marlon?" David asked.

"Dirk said no one ever just says what he's got right off. Got to let it flow, right?"

"Perhaps," David said. He wasn't sure what the kid was talking about, but Marlon went to the kitchen and found the gin and the cocktail shaker and two V-shaped glasses, ice in the freezer. He worked confidently, apparently familiar with the ritual.

"Cheers," he said. The drink, the strength of it, made David's eyes open. He could feel a pulling in his cheeks.

"I like these glasses," Marlon said, "how you tip 'em to your lips and the liquor slides right in."

David nodded, waiting.

"It's good, right? Everyone says I make a good martini. I've done some bartending here and there. Private clubs, you know."

"It's an honest living, bartending."

"Yeah, that's why I wanted to talk to you."

"Okay."

"Remember before you said I could change my life."

"I do."

"Yeah. I've been thinking, maybe you're right. Maybe I can change. It's not like I grew up wanting to do this. Thought maybe I'd get me a real job, stop worryin' 'bout everything. Live like a civilian."

"It sounds like a great idea. Dirk would be happy."

"Dirk, man, it was never all that easy to make him happy, you know."

"I didn't really know him," David said.

"You just live in his house."

"I *bought* the house."

"Yeah, and I got this idea about that."

"What idea?"

"Dirk told me I always had a place to go. Times got bad, I could come here."

"But Dirk's dead."

Marlon shrugged. He apparently thought that Dirk's promise extended beyond death, that the obligation—the covenant—stayed with the house, no matter the owner. "You want to live in my house?" David asked, to make sure he had it right.

"Just the guest room downstairs, like always. I'm quiet. I can help out. And it's good for you to have a brother living in the house, in this neighborhood."

"Marlon, you can't be serious." What, David wondered, actually went through this kid's mind?

"Serious? I'm serious. I need a place. Can't go back where I was."

"Why not?"

"Just believe me, I can't," Marlon said.

"You could live with your mother."

"You want to live with your mother?"

"You've got money," David said. "Get an apartment."

"You said you'd help me. That's why I'm asking for a little help. Show me some civilian stuff, like you did at the bank. I thank you for that, by the way."

"Civilian stuff."

"Yeah. No one's ever done that. I've learned a lot from you."

"I don't know, Marlon." David remembered his own father taking him to the bank to open an account. He'd been about twelve.

"I'll stay out of your way," Marlon said. "Besides, what are you gonna do with all this space? It would be good for you, you know, to have somebody in the house. Not good to live alone."

David took down his cell phone number. Marlon had a pay-as-you-go plan; the number was always changing. David walked him to the door, feeling dizzy from the drink, from Marlon's request.

"I'll think on it," he told Marlon. David couldn't decide if he was more taken aback by this bizarre request or by the fact that Marlon didn't seem to think it was anything special. It occurred to David that no one had needed anything from him in a long time.

"Even pay you rent," the kid said. David waited while Marlon slowly made his way out. Marlon took two steps from the door and then turned and waved. In that big jacket he looked like a little kid. David couldn't help but like him.

XVIII

THROUGH A FRIEND Carolyn had gotten an interview with an ad agency, and so earlier that day she had put on her business clothes—the skirt was too tight, but the jacket covered that up—and driven downtown. When she was a little girl her father had taken her down Woodward to the old Hudson's. Back then Woodward had been crowded with pedestrians, the street lit up with signs from stores and the streetlights themselves. People dressed up to shop at Hudson's. Now Hudson's was gone, and she was vying for the chance to pick at the dwindling marketing dollars left on the carcass of the Detroit auto business. The job paid roughly sixty percent of what she was making in L.A.

The interview was in the Penobscot Building, a structure grand enough to lift her mood. She stood in the lobby and looked at the art deco design of the floor and decided that the city didn't have to decline forever, that nothing was set in stone. Then she walked over to security and announced herself.

. . .

"TELL ME AGAIN," the interviewer said, "why you want to work in Detroit."

He was young, early thirties, she guessed, trying hard to look older. "Look, kid," she wanted to say, "you're young—don't fight that. Enjoy every goddamned fleeting minute."

She actually said, "It's my home."

"But twenty years in Los Angeles?"

"Training. Getting ready for this job."

He looked out the window, and she followed his gaze. They were looking north in winter, and it seemed that somewhere over gray Michigan there was a strip of blue sky, a tease. It was two days before Christmas, three after the shortest day of the year. Light was at a premium.

"I wouldn't want to work here," he said.

"But you do," she pointed out.

"Long lines of guys like me in New York and Chicago, but none here."

"So you've got your reasons, and I've got mine."

"The last two people we hired left inside a year. They both took jobs where it doesn't snow."

She began to understand that she could have the job if she would just say that she wanted it and she would stay. Of course, she'd need at least a year to really start. She didn't think it would matter. Everyone else wanted out.

"I like the snow," she said.

"Really? Why?"

"I miss it."

"Then why did you live in L.A. for twenty years?" he said.

"Lack of imagination," she said.

XIX

CHRISTMAS DAY AND Marlon was playing Call of Duty 4 with E-Call, shooting up Germans like nobody's business. It was fun, to a point, but it creeped Marlon out how E-Call got off on wasting the enemy, as if there were no life behind it. Which there wasn't. Still, when Marlon pretended, he pretended fully, till for him it was real.

Hiding from Elvis but hanging with E-Call was fraying his nerves, making him wake up thinking there was a gun pointing in his face. That was always a possibility. Elvis meant to kill him. He trusted E-Call—they were brothers, they went way, way back—but E-Call had worries of his own, lying to Elvis every damn day. If Elvis found them together, he'd kill the both of them. If Marlon took off, it would take some heat off E-Call. Marlon figured he owed his brother that much.

He got up to take a leak, stood over E-Call's ancient toilet, and thought of the guys he used to know who were gone, BB and Crick and Lionel, all dead, and Shocker, who took a bullet in the spine and was now stuck in a chair, shitting into a plastic bag, maybe even worse off than the other three. It was how things went and he'd known it all along, though lately he'd felt it more.

"How many gangsters make it to thirty, Marlon? Answer me that." Dirk had said this on the last night of his life. But that was in July, when thirty seemed far away and very old. Now, for some reason, it didn't.

"Gotta go," Marlon told E-Call when he got back from the can.

"Man, you sure took a long time in there. Where you going now?"

"Ypsi. My mom's."

"Why?"

"Christmas, man."

"See you on the flip side."

Marlon wanted to take E-Call to his mother's so E-Call didn't have to be alone. It was Christmas, and Marlon thought everyone should have a place to go. *I ain't coming back,* Marlon wanted to tell him, but he didn't. Easier for E-Call that way. No farewell. No knowledge that he'd have to keep secret. That was the best way—you just didn't show up. No goodbye but most definitely gone.

. . .

HE DROVE OUT I-94 to Ypsi. The road was damn near empty, except for some sorry-ass truckers who didn't have a better place to be than on the road. There was something sad about it. He thought again about how he should have brought E-Call, but he needed to let E-Call be and he wanted to keep his mother separate from the rest of his life. It was her best chance. Today she prepared one of her spectacular meals. After prayers and a couple gifts—he'd bought her an i-Pod and loaded it up with that old music she liked—they ate, almost in silence.

"Just want you to know, Mom, that from this day on, I'm going straight." He was at the sink now, helping her dry dishes, his stomach so full he was thinking he wouldn't eat tomorrow, the first day of his new life.

"That's good," she said.

"And I'm gonna get my GED."

"Your father always wanted you to go to college."

"I don't know about that. But the GED, I'll get that, just like Dad."

"The GED is a start," his mother said. "But fathers, they always want their sons to go further."

"Something the matter?" he asked, knowing there was; he could hear it in the way she talked, softly, as if she could barely get the words out.

She handed him a plate. "I worry," she said.

"I'm gonna be clean, get me a job, with hours and all. Solid-citizen stuff."

"What happened?" she wanted to know.

"I'm older, is all. Been remembering Dad, and Dirk, thinking maybe they were on to something. Sometimes, for me, it's like they're still here. Like ghosts or something. I had that feeling today, like I was going to walk in here and Dad would be washing up for dinner, scrubbing that steel plant off of him."

"I get that feeling sometimes, too," his mother said. She thought a moment and then wanted to know what kind of work he was going to look for.

"Bartending. I'm good at it."

"You'll be out late, when all the trouble happens."

"You worry too much," he told her. "Bartending you make good money, cash tips, and they got smoking outlawed pretty much everywhere now, so the air's good. Lot better than some steel plant. I can go to school in the day. I'll get further than Dad. You'll see, Mom."

With that his phone started ringing. She looked at him

as if she were accusing him; he looked down at the number: 303. Where the hell was that? Wasn't 313, Detroit, or
312, Chicago. He answered it.

"Marlon, it's David Halpert."

"Yo," Marlon said. "Give me a sec." To his mother he
said, "It's my lawyer."

"Why you need a lawyer? And what kind of lawyer
calls on Christmas?"

"He's the lawyer, how should I know?" Marlon set the
towel on the counter and made for the living room.

"I'm here," he said.

"Been thinking about your proposal," David said.

"You been thinking good," Marlon said.

"How's that?"

"You don't call a brother on Christmas to give him bad
news."

"You got me there, Marlon. But I've got conditions."

"Ground rules?" Marlon said.

"You could call them that," said David.

"Then tell me what you need."

XX

DAVID HUNG UP the phone and paced around his living
room. It was an impetuous decision, though maybe, he
thought, a mitzvah, a deed done because it needed to be

done and he could do it. It would be good to have someone in the house. Marlon was a black kid twenty years
younger, and maybe he could be good company. Certainly
he needed guidance.

Mostly David missed Cory. All the strain of fathering
seemed like nothing compared to not being able to do it at
all. It was a loss at the center of him, searing and eternal.
David knew he was looking for a second chance and that
he'd never really get one, not the exact one he was looking for. Still, other chances would come around, and he
intended to make use of them.

He found himself strolling along his bookcases, looking at the cloth spines of the books. "They're all Dirk's,"
Shelly had explained. "He collected books, could never
throw one away."

"And the covers?" David asked.

"I took them off. Didn't like the way they shined in the
light, all garish and cheap."

Now, at the end of a shelf, David noticed an envelope, and he pulled it out. Actually there were three, all
addressed to Dirk, "c/o The Bookers," in "Detroit, Mich."
There was no zip code. David checked the postmarks: 1958
and 1959.

David pulled a letter from one of the envelopes. It
started, "My dearest little boy," and it was signed, "Love,
Mommy." The script was odd, difficult to read. A letter
from Tina to Dirk.

David read all three. In the letters Tina professed her
love and lamented that they lived apart. It baffled David:

they were separated by just a few miles, and yet they had their own personal 8 Mile running right through the family.

David fetched a legal pad from his briefcase, sat in one of the living room's reading chairs, and wrote his own letter. "Dear Cory," it started.

> *I miss you as I would miss life itself.*
> *If I could be with you, then I would be*
> *with you. They say if you save one life*
> *you save the whole world. If I could have*
> *saved you it would have saved our world,*
> *yours and mine. But I couldn't. I am*
> *sorry about that, and mostly I am sorry*
> *about how I left things with you. I can't*
> *change that. But there is this one other*
> *life I can change, so I will. I am letting*
> *someone live in my house. He is a young*
> *man who needs a little help, and I am*
> *going to give it to him. Just as I would*
> *have given it to you.*
>
> *Love, Dad*

He folded up the note and slid it between two of the envelopes that contained Tina's letters. Then he put them all back where he found them, now his own personal Wailing Wall. He stepped back. It felt, oddly, as if the world had changed. And then the phone rang.

XXI

IT WAS STILL Christmas, and she was driving to the city to see David at Dirk's house. All the Christmases of her life she had never once visited it.

She'd called him and said that she had to see him right away, and of course he had agreed. It was time. She couldn't keep putting it off. Having the baby was her decision, and if he wanted nothing to do with the child, she would accept that. She would have to accept it, but she didn't want it to go that way. She also didn't want an offer of marriage—it was too soon, and she was still technically married, in any case. She just wanted him to accept the situation, to let her stay in his life, and he in hers, and to agree that somehow they would raise the child. She was asking for just one simple thing: the possibility of a future.

"Did someone die?" he asked when he opened the door. She entered the house. He looked exhausted. It was a little after ten. She had promised nine and was late, as usual.

"Honestly," he said, "I've been trying to come up with what you felt was so important that you had to come down here in the middle of the night on Christmas to tell me."

"Can we sit down?" she asked.

"Is it about Dirk?"

"What about him?"

"Have they found anything out? Anything about what happened?"

"They've got shell casings and slugs, but no guns that

match. They've gone through several dozen of his old cases to see if this was payback of some kind. People on parole, that sort of thing. They've found nothing."

"So they still have no idea?"

"No." Her feet were hurting. "Can we sit down?"

They went to the living room, where months before she had sat with her mother and Shelly and looked at the pictures of her dead brother. Now she sat and took a deep breath. She had practiced a preamble, but she dispensed with it. "David," she said, "I'm pregnant. With your baby."

He just stared at her, as if he couldn't believe what he'd heard. She wished he would say something. Anything. She had an odd feeling, as if she were about to be hit by lightning.

"I'm not asking for anything from you," she told him, and then she went into the speech she'd practiced in the car, how this had been her choice, she didn't want to pressure him into anything. She also felt he had the right to know, it was—

He held up his hand.

"Are you telling me you don't want me involved?"

"No," she said. "I'd like you involved. I'd really like it."

"Good."

There was a long silence. Why, she wondered, wasn't he saying anything? For a moment she wondered if he'd heard her, or if she'd said anything at all.

"That's all you're going to say?" she asked. "I mean, David, you and me, I've been thinking we've got a chance, you know, but then there's this baby, and that puts all this pressure on it. All this responsibility. I want to do it right, and I hope that I can do it right with you. But it's—"

"I had a son once," he said, cutting her off by changing the angle of his shoulders. "And I didn't think I'd ever have another. Of course I'll raise this child with you. How could you think otherwise?"

"It's soon for us. Maybe too much, too soon."

"I don't believe in that," he said.

"In what?"

"In too much, or too soon. There's either good or there's not good. There's either right or there's not right."

He smiled at her, stood, and walked to her. He held out his hand. She took it and he pulled her to her feet. He put his arms around her. He had a distinct smell, musky now, a man who lived hard, who tried hard. She felt his arms around her ribs. She leaned against him and he let her, holding her. This, she realized, was what she wanted, once in a while to put her weight in a man's arms. In all her years with Marty, never once had he done anything like this. She felt herself crying.

"It's right," he whispered.

"How can you know that?"

"You and me, Carolyn," he said, "we've got nothing to lose."

Summer 2006

I

When his phone started to shake, Dirk knew it was Marlon. Dirk had always had that sense; the two of them were connected in that way.

"Yo, Uncle Dirk, yo," the kid said.

"Two yo's too many," Dirk said.

"Just playing with you."

It was a sunny day, warm and humid, like most of July. He was out in his driveway, working on the car, moisturizing the leather in the front seat. Marlon didn't call to check in or to see how the Burtons were making out, and certainly not to invite them out for a meal or a get-together. Marlon called for one reason: he needed something.

"You need a place to go?" Dirk asked.

"You mean, like sleeping?" Marlon said. "Yeah, I was thinking I might use a few nights."

"Why don't you move in?" Dirk said. "Stay with us."

"That would be with your ground rules," Marlon said.

"You know the deal, if you're ready for it." Dirk had made this offer many times before. He made it as an offering to Everett, and he made it because, despite Marlon's poor behavior, he liked the boy and wanted to help him.

"Maybe," Marlon said.

Dirk dropped his rag, stood up in the sunshine. Marlon had never said "maybe" before. "Talk to me, son."

"Thought we could negotiate," the boy said.

"Negotiate? Negotiate what?"

"Ground rules. Like you call 'em."

"There's a reason they're called ground rules and not ground suggestions."

"Want to make sure we're communicating," Marlon said. This was one of Dirk's lines, coming back at him. Marlon did that often.

"They are my rules," Dirk said. He wanted to take Marlon in, but not if his house would be used as a base for a career in the drug trade. He'd spent his whole life fighting it, and there was some irony he just couldn't take. Not that he'd ever thought he'd win the long fight with the dealers, but he had won the short ones. His own survival was proof of his victory. Sooner or later all the drug dealers went away. That was certain. It was why he wanted to help Marlon get out before it was too late.

"I was just thinking at dinner we might get it all worked out," Marlon said. Dirk had also taught him this. It was why interrogations could take forever. No one just came out and said what he had to say. Often he had to say everything else first.

"Okay, dinner will work," Dirk said. "You need a ride?"

"I'm good on the ride. I was thinking Greektown." Marlon loved Greek food. And Lord knew the kid needed to eat.

"Greektown, then."

"Bring your sister," Marlon said.

"My sister?"

"The white girl."

"What for?"

Marlon had met Natalie on a chance encounter, down on the esplanade by Hart Plaza. Marlon had been up to no good, Dirk was sure. This was back in May, an evening with the same milky sky and warm air as now. "Meet my sister," Dirk had said at the time.

"Your sister?"

"Same momma."

"Damn," Marlon said.

"You're Everett's son," said Natalie. After that, Marlon changed, dropped the swagger and acted almost human, merely from hearing his father's name. Dirk had never felt that hearing his own father's name, but often fathers were like that, Dirk had noticed, both a burden and a blessing.

"Be good to have a third party there," Marlon said. He wanted Natalie to be the referee.

"You can trust me to do what I say I'll do. You know that."

"I'm just saying, you and me, we don't always see the world the same way," Marlon said. "She can be like the Judge Judy."

Dirk heard something off in Marlon's voice. "You in trouble?" he asked.

"I'm good."

"Seven, then." The line went dead. There was no mention of the restaurant, but they always went to the same place, the New Parthenon, right there in downtown Detroit.

Dirk slid the phone into his pants, looked up, and saw Shelly watching him from the front door. He knew himself to be a lucky man, and most of this was because of her. All these years and he was still in love with her. Even the passion he had felt for her at the beginning could still well up in him. They agreed on almost everything. There was really only one issue between them.

"Marlon," he explained.

"You don't have to be that boy's savior."

"Gotta try."

"Dirk, he's up to no good. You say it yourself."

"He wants to set himself right. I made a promise. I've got to help."

She walked down the front steps and over to his car, so she could speak softly. Beads of sweat dotted her forehead. "I don't think so."

"He's going to move in for a while." He wanted to tell her about the dinner tonight but decided not to. For Shelly he had to keep Marlon down to small doses. He said he was meeting Natalie, but Shelly wasn't through on the subject of Marlon.

"When you made that promise to Everett, he didn't mean this. Everett never would have asked this much."

"Everett asked only for what he needed. Look, baby, it's not much. A meal here and there, a phone call."

"A place to stay."

"He's a good guest. Quiet."

"Comes and goes at all hours. Never says goodbye."

"He's growing up," Dirk told her. "He'll get better. So please, let me keep my word."

.   .   .

HE PICKED UP Natalie at 6:15, and together they headed back south down the long corridors of Detroit freeway.

"How's it feel, playing judge?" he asked.

"I like it."

"Of course you'll be on my side."

"I'll be fair," she said.

"That's Marlon's idea about you."

"He's a good judge of character, then," she said.

Perhaps he was. Or perhaps he was learning. Marlon was twenty-five now. Street smart, no doubt. Dirk had worked these streets for more than twenty years, knew much of what the kid knew, which was a lot of crumbling, crime-soaked cement, vacant buildings, broken glass, depthless desperation and desire. The weak and the strong.

Lucky and unlucky. A sane man of a certain age—maybe it was twenty-five—would get out.

"So you understand," he told Natalie. "Marlon is trying to get out of the life, and this needs to happen. It's a fine line, laying down the rules and not scaring him back to the streets."

"Why does he want to live with you?"

"Lost his father young. I think he might be getting old enough to realize he could use some guidance. Also, something out there is scaring him."

"What is it?"

"I don't know."

"Then how do you know it's scaring him?"

"I've got an ear for it," he told her. "And I've been listening for a long, long time."

II

EARLY THAT MORNING Marlon parked his car by Greektown, but the day had taken him far afield and so now he had E-Call drop him at the Ren Cen. He didn't want E-Call to know he was meeting Dirk, whom E-Call called "Mr. FBI." Marlon said he had a dentist appointment, was going to see about some gold caps. Marlon knew it would never occur to E-Call that you don't go to the dentist after six at night, or that the Ren Cen wasn't the kind of place people got their teeth fixed.

"What's it like in there?" E-Call asked Marlon. Marlon just wanted to get out of the Mazda, which E-Call was proud of though it was really just a crappy car they'd taken off a junkie. It was shined to a black gleam, but it was still a Mazda.

"Ain't nothing," Marlon said.

"Damn," E-Call said. "I wouldn't go up there, all that glass."

Marlon shrugged. E-Call was scared of heights, didn't even like driving across the Ambassador Bridge.

Marlon decided to take the People Mover, just like old times. Lately he'd been feeling nostalgic, thinking almost every day about his father. In a way, Marlon was similar to E-Call, T-Bone, Ray-Ray—he didn't have a father. Unlike them, he knew where his father was. And he had Dirk. None of them had a Dirk. No one else, anywhere, had a Dirk.

At seven, summer nights were still bright, hazy with the humidity, Canada almost fuzzy across the water. Up here on the People Mover, a man could feel powerful. Marlon wondered what Dirk would think if he knew $43,000 was stashed between the floor joists in his guest bedroom. It had taken almost two years to skim the money, a twenty here, a Grant there. He'd converted all the bills to hundreds and hidden them in the floor. It was amazing when you saw it there, all in one place: forty-three grand hardly took up any space at all.

They knew, though. Maybe not who had the money or how it was disappearing, but someone above E-Call knew something. E-Call said so. Elvis wasn't happy. Of course, Elvis was never happy, except about his name, which he'd chosen himself. He thought it funny, a black man named Elvis. "No one in this crew better be skimming," E-Call said. "They find out it's one a us—hell, they even *think* it's one a us—we all dead."

It was getting to be a risk to stick around, and Marlon figured it was a good time to step out. They wouldn't find him. Palmer Woods was way out of the territory, and Marlon would go north into the white areas for work. He'd lie low till he didn't have to look over his shoulder. Once he was sure no one was looking for him, he'd head west. Start over, just like Dirk was always telling him to do.

And no doubt it was what his father would want. He wished he could talk to the man now. He wanted to know what he'd say. In the past, the answer was obvious: get an education and a job at a desk. "It's the way of the world, son," his father once said. "Sweat your ass off in some plant, you make a little. Sit at a nice desk, eat your lunch with silverware, you make a lot. You just need the diploma. It's the key to the kingdom." But now there were hardly any desk jobs left; it was a different world in Detroit. Out west, though, there was supposed to be opportunity. And schooling was cheap. So maybe the answer was the same, just not in Detroit.

Getting on the People Mover at the Ren Cen meant he got to do almost the full loop before he got to Greektown, not a bad deal for fifty cents, a loop that ran by Joe Louis and Cobo, up almost to the new stadiums, and then down to Greektown. Marlon was the only person he knew who'd ever been on the People Mover. It was something tourists did, like people from Warren or Southfield, white or black. They were around him now, and he noticed they kept their distance, gave him all the space he needed. *I ain't packin'*, he wanted to say, but even then he doubted they'd take the chance.

The restaurant had statues and fountains and waiters who lit cheese on fire and yelled "Opa!" Greece, he thought, must be one fucked-up place, but they ate well, better than cheeseburgers, and Marlon liked cheeseburgers. Marlon looked around: white folk mostly, and no Dirk or his sister. This was good, that he was first. It was advice he'd once heard Dre tell E-Call: you got a meet, you get there first. That way you could see what was coming at you.

Next thing Marlon knew, Dirk was hugging him, that whole big body and that cologne Dirk wore covering him like a blanket. One thing about Dirk: he was a big dude, six-three, an old man now, like fifty or something, but still tough-looking. Mr. FBI, the undercover brother. The white sister, Natalie, just stuck out her hand. "Nice to see you again, Marlon," she said.

She was older but still a good-looking woman, and people kept looking over at the table, at this blond girl with the two black guys. It didn't bother Marlon much; he was used to getting stared at in the nice parts of town. He waited it out while the conversation went through stories of Dirk growing up with Marlon's father and the crazy things they did when they were young, which weren't really all that crazy, since what scared them most was getting caught by Marlon's grandfather and that just wasn't scary. At one point Marlon went to the john so he could check his text messages—the phone had been vibrating in his pocket—and he found three from E-Call. Jackson had been shot at, maybe some turf war crap, but maybe just the kind of random thing that happened now and again. Nonetheless, Elvis had everyone on high alert. Marlon called E-Call. He didn't want E-Call coming to look for him.

"What's that mean?" Marlon asked. "High alert."

"Means watch your back."

"I ain't working tonight, remember?"

"You think these motherfuckers care you're working?"

"How's Jackson?"

"He fine," E-Call said. "How them caps?"

"Don't have 'em yet. Gotta go." Marlon hung up. Marlon had known E-Call as long as he could remember, back when they were in maybe the second grade, drawing cars they'd make when they got older. Soon Marlon would move out of his life. Not seeing his friend would make the world a different place, which was sad but had to be.

Back at the table they got down to it. What Dirk wanted was simple. Marlon had to have a full-time job, pay three hundred bucks rent ("So you know it's worth something to live there," Dirk said), and not stay out past midnight.

"What am I, fourteen?" Marlon said. "Midnight?"

"It's when all the trouble starts," said Dirk.

"What if I'm working?"

"That's different."

Marlon fumed. Then he thought, *Well, if I say I'm working, then I'm good.* "Fine," he allowed.

"You're doing the right thing," Natalie said.

"Funny how everyone is always thinking they know what that is."

"I got a good idea," she said.

. . .

AFTER DINNER THEY walked to Dirk's car, which he'd parked on the street. It was a sweet Mercedes, damn near new, just like he always had, this one with a white Olde English *D* on its back window.

"That for Dirk or Detroit?" Marlon asked.

"Must be Detroit," Dirk said. "This here is what they call a pre-owned vehicle. The last customer put that D on."

"How 'bout I take it for a spin?" Marlon asked. He said it like he was joking, but he hoped to get a yes. He just wanted that feeling, cruising neighborhoods in a fine car. He'd stay west, he decided, away from the trouble areas, streets where no one would take a shot at him. "Fifteen minutes," he said to Dirk.

Dirk looked at Natalie.

"Buy me dessert?" she said.

Dirk handed Marlon the key, which wasn't a key at all, just the thing you needed to get the engine to start. First thing, then, was to get the CD off and find a radio station;

you couldn't be cruising Detroit to that Motown Dirk liked as though it were still 1966. And then he was off, didn't leave any rubber in case Dirk was still watching. He drove south to the river, then a little west and up to a couple blocks he knew where there were a few bars and maybe a few girls who might want a ride. He ran the AC but kept the window down and the reading light on so he could be seen, and damn if the first person who called to him wasn't Elvis. Told him to stop.

Elvis was scary because he never, ever showed anything that might be construed as human emotion. Never laughed or chuckled or even smiled. Worse, as E-Call said, you never saw him mad. "That's scary," E-Call said. "You never see a dude when he's mad, how you gonna know when you got a situation?"

Marlon felt he had one now.

"What is this?" Elvis said, dry as sawdust.

"What?" He was pulled to the curb on the wrong side of the street, facing into traffic. Elvis had this one scary beast with him, a guy Marlon knew but had never spoken to. This was Dre. Marlon never dealt directly with either one. E-Call did that and it frightened him, and that was good enough reason for Marlon to stay away.

"This is how you're on high alert?"

"I thought here, on the West Side—"

"And you're driving a 500 Series now? Where'd you get that bank?"

"Sixty grand easy," said Dre.

"It ain't mine."

"Detroit nigger shouldn't be driving no foreign car," Dre said.

"It ain't yours. You stole it, you're saying," said Elvis.

"It's my uncle's." As soon as the words were out, Marlon knew they were a mistake. Saying he stole it was the right answer. The truth was dangerous.

"*You*," Elvis said, "got a rich uncle."

Dre smiled. Behind Elvis and Dre, people walked up the sidewalk but didn't look over, which wasn't normal. People knew Elvis, and no one wanted to witness anything.

Marlon tried to explain. As proof he put on the CD player, and some raspy guy started singing about a girl named Bernadette.

"See," Marlon said. "It's my uncle's. I wouldn't be listening to that ancient-school shit."

"You making fun of Levi Stubbs?"

"Who?"

"Where'd you get the money for this car?" Elvis wanted to know.

"It ain't my car," Marlon pleaded.

"I can find you."

"It ain't my car."

Elvis just stared, and Marlon felt like he might piss himself. He looked straight ahead and whispered to the dash, "It ain't my car." It wasn't right. There was nothing wrong with borrowing a car. If shit went down now, over this . . .

Then, ahead, he saw a cop car turn onto the street. The car came right at him, then flashed its lights. A loudspeaker said, "Move it. Get on the right side of the road."

Marlon pulled out without looking back. At first he couldn't breathe, and then he was gasping. He headed straight back to Greektown. He turned up the AC and tried to flutter his shirt. His hand was shaking. It took a moment to get a grip on his shirt. It was sticking to him, wet as if he'd been caught in a downpour.

III

THEY SAT AT the wooden bar, eating baklava and drinking coffee, Dirk's left arm resting on the counter. His skin was a rich café au lait color. Natalie stared at the hair on that arm, curly and black.

"Why'd you start shaving your head?" she asked him.

He patted the stubble. "It isn't shaved."

"Close."

"Yeah, well, I'm close to bald. Doesn't look too bad, does it?"

"No," she said, and she meant it. He was a handsome man, with or without hair.

"Shelly says she likes it like this."

"You two still . . ."

"Yeah," he said. "We still . . . Whatever 'still' is. Couldn't imagine my life without her. But she's talking about moving."

"Where to?"

"Texas." Natalie knew Michelle was down there, no doubt hoping her parents would keep their distance. Natalie remembered being in her twenties. She should have moved away, like Carolyn did. That was the smart move.

"So go," she said.

"To Texas? I'd be out of my mind. I already live in a palace. I told Shelly, we can visit as much as she wants. Shelly, she doesn't like the snow. Me, I like it."

"Why?"

"Well, for one, I know it. Two, I like change, the seasons. Leaves, then colors, then no leaves, then snow, then leaves again. A man can feel the world spinning."

"Like he's running in place?"

He smiled at her. "Could have used you when I was growing up, sister."

"Me?" she said.

"Someone to tell me I'm full of it," he said. She was fairly sure he meant this as a compliment. He often joked with her, and she rarely could decide whether it was with her or at her expense. It was his way. Growing up, she'd always wanted an older brother, and had had no idea she actually had one.

Dirk looked out the window. "Where's that boy at?"

"Marlon?"

"Anyone else got my car?"

"Trying to impress some girl."

"A girl that rides with you 'cause of your car will take other rides, too."

"You ever taught that to Marlon?" she asked.

He turned to her. "I've tried to teach him everything I know. Promised his father. It's not easy. I push too hard, I never see him. I let him do what he wants, he runs wild. I can't win with him."

"You've done all right," she told him.

"Why do you say that?"

"He's here tonight. So you've made a difference."

"I used to tell myself if I saved one kid, just one, then it was enough. Just one."

"Don't shrug like that," she told him. "It's true."

"No," he said. "We tell ourselves lies because we need the justification. The purpose. But I know different now. It's not enough. Not anymore."

. . .

She thought he was wrong. Change one life and you've justified your own. She couldn't think of a single person whose life she'd made better. Henry, her father's old partner, for whom she still worked, said he couldn't live without her, but she was sure he could go out and find someone to run his office. There wasn't a man who couldn't live without her. And there were no children. Who out there really depended on her, now or ever? So maybe that was where the meaning was.

Marlon walked in the door looking like hell. He'd nearly sweated through his T-shirt, and his brow was wet and clammy. The look of him brought Dirk out of his chair.

"You all right?"

"Yeah, fine. Car's out front. Got a spot right on the street."

"What happened?" Natalie asked.

Marlon looked at her as if he'd never seen her before. "What you mean?"

"You're all sweaty."

"It's hot out."

"That car has air conditioning," Dirk said. "I left it on, in fact."

"I drive with the windows open. Like the fresh air." He put the key in Dirk's palm. "So, we're done."

"You're making the move," Dirk said.

"Tomorrow," Marlon said. "The afternoon, like."

Dirk smiled and then did something Natalie didn't expect. He reached forward so quickly she thought he was grabbing Marlon, as if to keep him from getting away, as if he were trying to control the young man. The way you'd control a criminal. Instead he just hugged Marlon, sweaty as he was. It was a sight. Dirk was three or four inches taller and much thicker. He whispered something in Marlon's ear, and Marlon nodded. She thought Marlon might be shaking, that he might even cry, but he didn't. When Dirk released him, Marlon turned to her.

"Yo," he said.

"Yo yourself," she said back. He smiled. *God,* she thought, *he's really young.* He walked out into the night.

Dirk waited a moment, then walked to the front window and looked out. Natalie followed. "Just checking on the car," Dirk said. They went back to the counter to get the bill. He was a hell of a man, her brother. Every time she was with him, she saw it. Whatever came his way, he just handled it.

"What did you say to him?" she asked.

"I told him that I believed in him, that I had always believed in him, that I would always believe in him, and that I was just waiting for him to prove me right."

"And what did he say back?" she asked.

"He promised it won't be long now."

IV

HE WALKED OUT into the night air thinking what he'd do for Shelly. Marlon staying for good would require a grand gesture—a trip to the islands in January, say. It was money he didn't really have—"Touching principal," Arthur would have called it, and it was Arthur's principal—but he'd spend it. That was also something he'd learned: that when you had to pay, it was better to pay early.

It was a warm night, weather he loved. He loved all weather, even the frigid winter air of a December night, but there was something truly special about the night air in summer, warm and humid but not too hot. He walked twice around the car, looking for damage. He found none. Satisfied, he helped Natalie with her door and got in himself, turned the engine over as he turned down the volume on the stereo. He was amazed to find that Marlon had left the stereo off. It wasn't how Dirk had left it, but it was a good sign. The kid was taking responsibility, thinking about people other than himself.

Natalie didn't want to go home. "Not yet," she said. "Show me Detroit, your Detroit."

"At night?"

"It's the time we've got."

He knew better, but he also knew the city. He'd avoid the truly horrendous spots. First he took her to the old Booker home. The house was still there, but he was surprised to find it had been abandoned, the windows knocked out, the grass in front nothing but weeds and brambles, the roof half gone, with gaping holes open to the night sky. A corpse of a building.

"That's where I grew up," he said. "With Marlon's father. But everything's gone in this city. Even if you still live here, you can't go back and see where you came from. This was a neighborhood once." There wasn't a light on the street, or movement of any kind. Dirk opened his window, and the sound of crickets flowed in. He'd last been here two years ago, and someone had been in the house.

"It's sad," she said.

"It is what it is."

"Carolyn says I should move out to California."

"You should go. But I don't know that I could take myself seriously in California."

"You ever been?"

"Afraid to go," he told her, and he was. Most of his

working life he'd pretended to be something he was not. He was fifty-two years old now and was through with that. He knew who he was, and places like California worried him. What if he got there and found he wasn't that person?

"What are we listening to, exactly?" she asked.

"The Four Tops. They're also part of my Detroit."

They drove back south to Wayne State. He'd gotten a football scholarship to Western Michigan, but instead he'd decided to rough it out at Wayne because it was a better school and he didn't want to play football for the privilege of his education. There was something abusive about the idea.

"Most guys would have been flattered," Natalie said.

"You're working for the university," he said.

"You're playing football."

"I was in a hurry."

"To work for the FBI?"

"To be my own man." That was all. He had relied on others for so long—his whole life—and he wanted to be beholden only to himself. He'd worked in the library shelving books. Libraries were full of almost nothing but books back then, and he liked the job because he liked books. There was pleasure in handling them, their texture, that odd musty smell when he opened a book that hadn't been touched in years. When he married Shelly and she wanted their library to be without dust jackets, he'd felt right at home.

"There was a bar there," he said on Cass, pointing to a dark storefront. "Probably our main hangout."

"Who's we?"

"Some of my friends—you know, the overserious, never-going-to-smile black students. I was president of that society. Fighting segregation in the streets, practicing it in the cafés."

"You wouldn't let whites sit with you?"

"None tried," he said.

"I would have."

"Maybe, sister. But you're family."

"I would have liked to hear you explain that to your black never-going-to-smile friends."

"They'd have been okay with it, maybe."

"Maybe?"

"Look," he said, "I've got a white family, and I've got a black family, so I can tell you this: black people are pretty much like white people, except for one thing—black people got to deal with white people. And that changes you."

They moved south, all the way to the river. "The Ren Cen was going up then," he said. "That was supposed to be the renaissance."

Something caught his attention when he turned off Gratiot. Headlights, changing lanes when he changed, as if he were being followed. He drove testing them, and sure enough, there was someone back there, fucking with him. First he thought it was some racist nut pissed that a black man had a Mercedes with a white woman in it, but the windows were tinted, and at night especially it was impossible to see inside. Had to be somebody who knew him. Some guy from the Bureau, like Turner, who never could

get it through his head that Dirk had left of his own voli-
tion, that he really didn't want to be back on the job. There
were those—more than a few—who thought he'd fucked
up big-time, something they didn't know about, and he
was allowed to resign, hush-hush, because he was black.
There was a time in his life when that would have driven
him half-crazy, but he was older now, and half over it.

He tried to lose the tail without committing any major
traffic violations—he had enough tickets—but they stayed
with him. Only Turner was that much of an asshole. He'd
think this was funny. It had to be him.

"What are you doing?" Natalie asked.

"Some guy I know is trying to mess with me. I'm just
trying to do a little messing back."

"Who?" She turned, looked out the back window.

"Guy I know, I'm pretty sure. Knows the car. FBI type
wanting to have fun."

He squealed the tires around a turn.

"This is fun?" Natalie asked.

"For men," he replied.

The song changed to "Standing in the Shadows of Love."

He was flying now, not ever sure what cross street he
was on, but up ahead he could see Cass. He slammed on the
brakes and pulled over to the side of the street, thinking
that Turner would decide that was enough and go right by
him, but the Charger—that's what it was—pulled right up
behind him.

The Charger was one of those cars the brothers used
when they wanted to buy American. There were all sorts

of weird ideas in this city. Why they'd give it to a white guy like Turner was a mystery. Anyone would make him. Dirk looked in the rearview mirror but couldn't see in the car. There was a .38 under Natalie's seat.

"Move your legs to the right," he told her, and then he reached under and pulled it out, leaving it on the floor by her feet, just in case. He turned down the music. If the maniac back there wasn't Turner but happened to be a cop and he asked Dirk to get out of the car, Dirk didn't want the gun in plain sight. Still, he wanted it close.

"This guy's your friend?" Natalie asked.

At that moment he was sitting back up from placing the gun at her feet and then he realized he never should have taken his hand off it. There were men standing at both windows, pointing guns in the car. There wasn't time to go back for the gun. He reached for the gearshift, and time slowed almost to a stop. It took forever for his hand to move the shift, and then the first bullet came through and hit him in the left shoulder, a burning tear, and Natalie screamed, he was turned that way and he had a thought, the first time he'd ever had it, that Natalie actually looked a little like his mother back when he was a little boy and how he had had two mothers, one white and one black, but also really no mother at all, and how he wished it could have gone a different way.

2007

I

David turned onto his street and suddenly it was spring. It appeared just that fast. The buds on the trees were expanding to catch the expanding light, and today, a few days after tax day, it was going to hit sixty-six, a new high for the year. Or so they had promised on WCSX. Now they were playing an old Amboy Dukes tune. David had his window down, and someone, he noticed, had just cut grass. Was there a better mnemonic device than smell? Better yet, the smell of grass? One whiff and he found himself trying to bring back every spring of his life, and they all seemed to come from his youth: standing in the outfield with Brady Johnson during batting practice, chasing his dog Lucky as Lucky chased a squirrel, walking with Natalie, his hand in her back pocket, as they left the school after a sudden heavy rain, night crawlers twisting on the cement sidewalk.

He thought his move back to Detroit was the best decision he'd ever made. The world seemed to be opening up for him just as those buds were opening on the trees. He parked his car in the driveway and took two steps toward his front door when he heard his name called. Before he turned, he tried to imagine who it was. Last week someone had yelled "cracker" at him, which was how he learned the term was still in use.

This time it was Russell Wilson, the retired judge, his neighbor. David had eaten dinner with the Wilsons twice at their home, each time apologizing that he couldn't reciprocate because he simply couldn't cook. He was still trying to find a way to repay them for their kindness.

"Marlon here?" Russell asked. He was wearing a tracksuit with a stripe down the side, as though it might be 1977.

"He's working."

"What's he do?"

"Tends bar out in Farmington."

"You've got to be careful with that boy," Russell said.

"I'm careful by nature," David said.

"I don't think you are. And neither is Marlon. He's always run wild. I know Dirk tried to look after him, but it never seemed to do much good. And if Dirk couldn't do it, well . . . Look, tell me this: why'd you take him on?"

"He asked for help," David said.

"You help everyone who asks, just like that?"

"I thought I could make a difference."

"I thought I could, too," Russell said. "Mostly, though, I put hoodlums like that kid away. You think you can change some little part of the world, but really? One man is just one man, and it happens rarely."

"Why are you telling me this?"

" 'Cause I like you. You're quiet and responsible, even if underneath you're crazy as they come. You remind me of myself at a younger age. What are you, about forty?"

"Forty-six."

"Trouble follows Marlon. Remember that."

"Seriously, Russell, what could happen? He's going to what, steal my wallet? There's nothing of real value in the house. The car's insured."

"I sat on the bench for thirty-one years. You would not believe what people get up to. You never know what will happen. You truly have no idea. All I know is that when bad things happen to someone, it's usually because he ran into the wrong guy."

"Marlon is not going to want to stay with me much longer."

"You just be careful," Russell said.

David followed Russell's eyes across the street, where two kids were starting up a game of catch. He guessed they were part of the same crew he'd seen playing football on Thanksgiving. It made David smile. He had always liked how the sports changed with the seasons.

"You like baseball?" David asked.

"Sure."

"That's it, then. Instead of dinner, let me take you and Susan to a game at Tiger Stadium."

"Susan won't want to go, but I'd love it. There's only one problem."

"What's that?"

"They play at Comerica now."

"Comerica, then. I'll get tickets."

• • •

Inside he changed out of his suit and sat in his reading chair with a legal pad. It had been four and a half weeks since he'd written to Cory. He dated the top of the page, gave it a tap with his pen, and then wrote, "Dear Cory." He tried to clear his mind of Stuart LeBlanc and his estate plan, of his father's latest request (a trip together to Chicago), of Russell Wilson's warnings. He wrote:

> It's April and the trees are sprouting
> leaves now, the grass is green, life is
> starting over. I'd like to take you to a
> Tigers game. We could sit and eat hot
> dogs and root for the Tigers. Not the
> Rockies, I know, but the Tigers have
> history, players we now know will never
> be forgotten. Ty Cobb. Hank Greenburg.
> Even Mark Fidrych. Grampa once took
> me to see him pitch. The place was

packed, people cheering every pitch, as though it were a World Series game. And the Tigers won.

Marlon's been here a little over three months. We don't see each other much. He works till two in the morning. I'm asleep when he gets home, he's asleep when I go to work. On the weekends we drink coffee in the kitchen. His is mostly milk and sugar. Not how I would take it, but when you get older you tend to like things less sweet.

In less than a month you'll have a little brother. I think I've forgotten what it's like to have a newborn in the house. When you were born I used to wake almost every hour and go to your crib, lean my head by yours, just to make sure you were still breathing. I guess I'm admitting I didn't know how to be a father. But, then again, what man does?

It's springtime. If you were here now, we'd be looking at colleges. This would be exactly the time that all the possibilities would be opening.

I miss you more than I can say.

Love,

Dad

He folded the page into the size of a letter and slid it into his spot between the books. It was the fourth letter. Now he had more than Dirk had saved from his mother. He pulled the old letters out and decided he shouldn't keep them, he should really give them back to Tina. Carolyn was coming over tonight, and that's when he'd pass them along.

II

SHE FOUGHT WITH Kevin: he didn't want to wear a coat. "Do you know how warm it's going to be today, Mom? Sixty-six!"

Four months in Michigan and the kid thought sixty-six was warm.

"Well, it's thirty-six right now. Wear your coat." She handed it to him. He took it in his left hand, hoisted his backpack over his right shoulder, and headed out the door. She couldn't see his eyes, but he was no doubt rolling them. Clouds of breath rose above his head.

"Put it on," she called.

"I'm gonna miss the bus." And he was gone.

She walked back to the kitchen table, though "walk" was really a euphemism. She wasn't walking anymore. It was more of a fat-man waddle, legs apart, spine tilted back to help carry the medicine ball that now protruded from her stomach. "End of April," the doctor promised with the kind of certainty that made her think he was wrong. The older she got, the less she trusted experts.

She could smell Kevin's cereal bowl, the sugary milk there. She lifted it and drank straight from the bowl. She'd been doing this daily, one of the odd habits she'd picked up, like never answering the phone till the third ring. Her mother didn't have caller ID, and waiting somehow made it easier not to know who was on the other end of the line. Something about her pregnancy made her crave control. Control was an illusion, she knew, but it was a necessary illusion, and so she created it for herself just the way some people did with God. Same impulse, she guessed.

But still she prayed. She wasn't very good at it, but there were things she wanted: Kevin's happiness; a healthy baby; true love. It's a short list, she said to God. She realized how much he'd already provided—health and the physical comforts, her current pregnancy notwithstanding. Kevin's happiness seemed within reach. He'd adjusted well, had half a dozen close friends, found the horrible Michigan winter the greatest novelty of his life. One morning last month he'd sat at the breakfast table and said, "You know what, Mom? There are different kinds of snow. Sometimes it's slushy, sometimes you can pack it, and sometimes it's sugary. It's amazing." Her son, she realized now, knew what she knew. They were that much closer in this small way.

She was old to have a baby, but the doctor had done every test there was and assured her everything was normal. Normal, she thought, was supposed to be a comfort.

It was how we bargained with ourselves. Well, she would know in a little over a month. At least know something.

As for love, well, she questioned if she'd ever really known it, beyond what she felt for Kevin, which was deep and always urgent but not, she thought, what women felt for their men. What she felt for Kevin was superior in every way, on a higher plane. But she was thinking lower now. Sometimes she wondered if passion was even possible. Maybe it was a passing, ephemeral thing, a flash glimpsed now and again. And yet Natalie had led a passionate life. Carolyn was sure of it. Even when her affairs ended badly—and they always did—it wasn't for lack of passion. Natalie was ready, always willing to take a chance. That appetite for risk—it was a gift.

She had felt passion many times with David. Still, there were always things in the way. She'd been married when she met him, and now, eight months into her pregnancy, she felt frightened to feel so much for one person. When they weren't together she wished they were, and there were times beside him when she felt she loved him as she had never loved a man. There were little things that moved her: the way he looked at her, straight on, without blinking, or the way he helped her from her chair, or the way he teased her, always keeping her a little off balance. It was all too much at once. She would have his baby and see where she was.

• • •

KEVIN CAME HOME from school with his jacket stuffed in his backpack, half of it hanging out, one sleeve swinging to and fro. He wanted to go to Burger King.

"Grandma's going to have dinner for you in a couple hours," she told him.

"Where you going to be?"

"I'm having dinner with David."

Kevin shrugged. He seemed to have no opinion about David one way or the other, and she was thankful for this miracle of teenage self-absorption.

"I just want to go," he said. "I'm not really going to eat."

"Then why go?"

"Some friends will be there. We're just going to, you know, kick it."

"Kick what?"

"It's an expression, Mom."

As a girl, she'd done the same thing. The Burger King had since been remodeled, but it was the same building. She remembered the excitement of sliding into a booth with her girlfriends, away from her parents, looking across the booths for boys, feeling the cool plastic on her legs that somehow suggested the possibility of all that could happen in her life.

She drove him there. He wore his shirt untucked, his shoes untied, his pants hanging low on his butt. She hated the look, but she didn't fight it: it was the style now. When they got to the parking lot he asked for five dollars.

"I thought you weren't going to eat," she said, but she fished the money out of her purse and handed it to him. He thanked her but didn't get out of the car.

"Man, Mom," he said. "I just gotta say, you are huge." Then he was gone.

She drove behind the building, around the cars waiting for drive-through—endless hunger here at 4:15 in the afternoon—and then to the other side of the building, where she hoped to get a glimpse of Kevin with his friends. This was the most dangerous time. He was a teenager now. Things could break in any direction. She thought for a moment of Anita Blackburn, one of her closest friends from fifth grade. By eighth Anita had a small tattoo and an appetite for any drug she could get. She dyed her hair coal black, walked the school halls listening to a Walkman, spent her free time smoking in the "smoking lounge," a square slab of cement out the back of the high school, open to the elements. Carolyn's junior year she passed it daily on her way to chemistry—it was off the science hall, of all places—and one day she went out to talk to Anita. This was February, maybe ten degrees, and Anita was out there in a short jeans jacket.

"Aren't you freezing?" Carolyn asked—their first words in three years.

"Turn around," Anita said.

Carolyn turned and watched the students pass the glass doors. It was a steady parade of well-dressed and well-fed kids, and from here Carolyn could see the sameness of it, the girls with their frozen, feathered hair, the boys

in jeans and hooded sweatshirts. Carolyn had been swimming in that current for three years but saw it now for the
first time.

"It's colder in there," Anita said.

Come spring Anita had left school, and Carolyn still
didn't know where she'd gone. She hadn't yet known that
people would come and go from her life like that. She asked
a few people about Anita and they looked at her as though
they couldn't understand why she cared.

•   •   •

She slowed by the windows on the north side of the
Burger King. She wanted a glimpse of Kevin. The sight
in the window made her breath catch. It was Natalie, the
blond hair with its slight wave, the set of her shoulders and
tilt of her head. A car honked. She pulled over to the side
and then got out of her car and walked toward her sister.
Natalie turned, aware perhaps of some movement outside.
It wasn't her. This woman had a flat nose and slightly lopsided face and brown eyes. She wasn't even a real blonde.
She looked at Carolyn through the window as though she
might be scared. Carolyn turned, embarrassed, wondering
what had frightened this woman. Could anyone be frightened by someone so huge and pregnant?

She got back into the car to collect herself. For a moment
she had truly believed she was looking at her sister. There
was no logic to it, but she had felt it deeply. Natalie was
still out there, haunting as ever.

III

"YOU'RE A YOUNG KID," Les told him. "You're used to staying up late. But wait till you get up there in years. I'm thirty-two in three months, and I tell you, this job is wearing on me."

Marlon nodded. One thing he'd noticed, anyone older was always telling him how good he had it, and yet he always seemed to be working for them. Here he was now, polishing glasses while Les gave his nightly sermon. Marlon didn't want to hear about being tired; he wanted to learn to mix drinks, work a bill. The other stuff—an easy smile, the gift of gab—he had if he needed it.

Marlon usually went home with a hundred bucks. Chump change, but at least he was an honest chump. It was all part of the plan. He knew they'd been looking for him, but where would they look? None of the brothers came into Farmington, at least none Marlon knew. Eventually they would lose interest. All Marlon had to do was keep his head down and wait for Elvis to die. He had no doubt it would happen. He hoped E-Call would make it. They went back, had history. It was E-Call who told him that he had to get lost, that Elvis wanted his head and kept asking E-Call about him. E-Call could have turned him in and gotten major props for it, but he didn't.

"You should leave, too," he'd told E-Call. "It's only a matter of time. Probably not a lot of it." E-Call had shrugged, exhaled an "I'm aw-ight," and looked away. That is, he'd heard it. Probably he'd been thinking about it. As for Elvis, well, Marlon figured no one stayed at that level long, never more than three years, and Elvis was in over two. It was just like Dirk always said. A new guy took over, sure he was smarter than the last, and it was never true.

It was E-Call's warning that made him wonder about Dirk and the sister, if Elvis had something to do with it. Elvis had seen Marlon in that car. They might have tailed him. Still, it was hard to imagine Dirk getting taken so easily. He knew how to handle himself. He was older, but the kind of guy you didn't run into often: he never bragged, and yet he was so sure of himself that you knew he would come out on top. If Elvis had killed him, then Marlon didn't want to know. Dirk used to say, "It's all over but the crying." Now Marlon understood what he meant.

Marlon wanted Dirk back. For a long time he had thought Dirk was crazy, or at least silly, the way he worked so hard and got so little for it. Of course, Marlon's father had been like that, too. The two of them had jobs they knew would never get them anywhere, at least nowhere with money. It seemed almost un-American, not wanting more, staying away from even a hint of showiness. These were men who didn't know the meaning of the word "bling," who stayed with one woman. They did it all in the same rundown place and never complained about it.

I must be getting older, Marlon thought, because Dirk's life, or even his father's life, didn't sound so bad, at least the solid-citizen part, the part with a job on the right side of the law, with a boss who might one day fire you but would never kill you. Bad shit was what everyone thought happened to someone else, despite all the damn bodies and beatings and general mayhem. Something in the game made you blind. No one inside could see that you won by walking away before you lost.

So he just had to wait on Elvis. He read the *Free Press* crime section every day and spent his nights as Les's barback, with his eyes often glued to the door. He didn't want to be surprised. Les had noticed, thought he was looking for women, which in truth was a small part of it.

· · ·

L.A. WAS THE plan, but he didn't want to leave town not knowing if Elvis was alive or at least in prison. In Los Angeles—"swimming pools and movie stars," as E-Call was always saying—he would never know if he was really on the run. He'd spend years looking over his shoulder. In Detroit he could learn a trade, wait for the news to find him, and then head west without a worry and maybe by then about fifty grand on top of what he had in the bank. In the meantime he had David, who could teach him what he needed to know about the world of civilians.

For instance, he'd just filed a tax return. His first one. One Saturday morning David had taken him to the post office and taught him how to send a letter so he'd get proof that the government got it. There was all sorts of shit out there like that, stuff he knew nothing about. He was beginning to understand how important this knowledge was.

"Now you're a law-abiding citizen," David had said outside the post office.

"Damn," Marlon responded, the only thing he could think to say.

•   •   •

IT WAS THE middle of the shift on Thursday when Monique came into the bar. He saw her the moment she put a high heel into the room. It bothered him how black mothers were always giving their girls these French names when there was nothing French about them, unlike, say, Marlon's own mother, whose family had actually come from a place where they spoke French. Monique looked good, though, better even than the last time he'd seen her, back in high school. Seven years. He figured they were probably the best years a woman was going to get. She was perhaps taller now—or maybe it was just the heels—and she had this wave to her hair. He tried to remember why he'd broken it off.

She was with a tall guy in a sport coat and an open collar, an older man who immediately made Marlon jealous. Looked like some guy with an office job and a nice car, making money no one would kill him for. The truth was they really didn't even stand out if you overlooked the skin color, which, of course, no one would overlook. Usually Marlon was the only black person in the room, and he was sure everyone knew it.

He wanted to talk to her, but he decided to stay low and

hope she wouldn't notice him. Hard to disappear if old girl-friends were finding you. No, he decided, she'd notice him, but maybe she wouldn't recognize him. He was two inches taller, and he wore his hair tight now. He was wearing a business uniform—black pants with a belt, white shirt buttoned all the way up, with a clip-on bow tie, like one of those Farrakhan freaks—and sometimes when he looked in the mirror he barely recognized the face staring back at him. There was a good crowd tonight.

A half hour later Laurie was yelling at him as he was stocking the bar's small fridge with more Buds from the back walk-in. He was kneeling but being careful not to let his knees hit the floor mats. He could smell them, that peculiar, funky odor of wet rubber.

"Hey, Marlon, there's a girl over on seventeen says she knows you." Laurie was the cocktail waitress, long legs and short hair.

"What girl?" he said, so he could finish the stocking.

"What girl you think?"

He stood. Monique was looking right at him.

"Damn," Les said, shaking up a cosmo, "you black people really do all know each other."

"I think I gotta go over there," Marlon said.

"I think you do," answered Les.

Marlon ducked under the bar counter at the end and walked to Monique's table, Monique smiling at him the whole way. Back in high school she was always telling him he could be somebody, that he was smart enough to do what he wanted, and the funny thing was, he thought she believed this. It wasn't just something she said.

"Well, look at you, Marlon Booker," she said now. She stood and hugged him, then introduced her date, whose name was Michael McKinley. He had a self-consciously firm handshake and a voice that he lowered to say, "How do you do?"

Marlon thought he knew why Monique was so happy: here she was, a customer at this out-of-the-city bar, and here Marlon was, *working* at that bar. Like she'd risen and he hadn't. He played along. "You living out in the burbs now?"

"We are," she said. "Michael and I are engaged."

"That's great," Marlon said, though he didn't like it. All this time, but he still thought of her as his.

"I'm glad to see you here," she said.

"Why's that?"

"I heard you were hustling, you know, downtown."

"Yeah? Who say that?"

"Just something going around. Thought I'd never see you again."

"You ever go back?" he asked. "To the east side?"

"Marlon, it's not like it's a different country."

"Feels it," Michael said. "Specially from this bar."

Marlon wasn't going to start liking this Michael dude, but the man had a point. "Listen," Marlon said to Monique, "you see anyone from the neighborhood, don't tell them you saw me."

"Why?"

" 'Cause I really don't want to be found."

She nodded, as if she understood. Which she didn't. He was glad to get back behind the bar.

IV

"YOU LOOK GREAT," he told her. She was standing in his doorway, a few weeks of pregnancy to go, with more weight in her face and an expression that seemed more serious. This felt earned, and David found it appealing. Many of the women he'd known seemed to believe that things would always work out for the best. David preferred a woman who faced the world head on.

"Don't bullshit me." She walked into the house.

"I mean it," he said. "Really great."

She studied him, gave him a look as if she might leave open the possibility that he was telling the truth. He led her to the living room, where he had her mother's letters on the side table. She sat, and he followed. He explained where he'd found the letters and handed them over.

"My God, it must have killed her," Carolyn said after she'd read them. "It might still be killing her."

He admitted it might still be.

"We have to do better," she said. She put a hand on his arm. "Promise me we'll do better."

"You could move in here," he said. "We could do better by being together."

"And send Kevin to Detroit schools?"

He hadn't thought of that. "We'll send him to Liggett," he said, wondering at the expense of a private school in Grosse Pointe.

"Where's that?"

"It's just out 8 Mile."

She considered, and didn't say no. This gave him hope. She said, "So, are you going to feed me? What are you making?"

"I don't cook. I'll take you anywhere you'd like."

She didn't want to go to a restaurant, she said, because then she would want a drink. "You want to make me happy?" she said. "Get me a Wendy's double bacon cheeseburger, fries, and a Frosty. You got a Wendy's around here?"

There was one up on 8 Mile and Livernois. He went to the drive-through and ended up waiting behind a Chevrolet pounding out rap. It was one of those times—there'd been a couple in the last several weeks—when he'd felt like a foreigner in his own city. Still, in the Audi (he still hadn't gotten the new car) he could feel the industrial pounding of the music, and it seemed a proper rhythm. He felt an ache for his city. Since moving back he'd found himself rooting for Detroit, reverently waiting for it to rise in some miraculous resurrection.

•　•　•

AT HOME HE watched as she devoured the burger as though she were a refugee from a famine-stricken land. He slid his burger her way.

"Aren't you hungry?" she asked.

"I don't know that I'm as hungry as you're hungry."

She tore off a corner of his burger and slid the rest back. "Yours always tastes better," she said.

Later she took him to his bedroom and made him turn off the lights. When Julie had been pregnant with Cory she hadn't let David anywhere near her, and till now Carolyn hadn't been that different. They hadn't slept together in more than a month. Tonight she lay on her side, back to him, and told him to put his arms around her. He could tell she was thinking; there was a certain tension in her body.

"You should move in with me," he said. "You and Kevin. All of us, the new baby, too, right here."

She didn't answer.

"Sometimes, Carolyn, you've just got to leap. You can't make a big move with baby steps."

"And you think I should make the big move."

"I do."

"Why?"

"Because I'm asking," he said.

V

MARLON DROVE HOME knowing the clock had been moved up. Like Monique wouldn't mention him the first time she ran into someone who knew him, or she'd put it on some stupid Facebook page. You could think the city was big and wide, but there were worlds within worlds, and they all touched. Word would get back to Elvis within a week.

He came in the house through the side door, walked past the pantry into the kitchen, and found David sitting with a cup of tea, the expensive kind where each bag came wrapped like a rubber in its own foil cover.

"You're up late," Marlon said.

"Or early."

He was wearing that blue robe he wore at night, which meant he was up late, or at least he hadn't bothered to get dressed yet.

"You okay?" Marlon asked.

"Couldn't sleep. You want some tea?"

"Tea's for, like, English people. I look English to you?"

David chuckled, got up, and went to boil more water. "You'll look English with a cup of tea," David said.

"You ever been to L.A.?" Marlon asked.

"Twice."

"You like it?"

"What's not to like? Sun and palm trees. Crowded, though."

"Been thinking I should move."

David finished playing with the tea bag and turned around. "L.A., huh?"

"I like the sun and I ain't never seen a palm tree."

David smiled. He was always doing that, which was odd, because Marlon didn't think David was all that happy. He put a cup of tea in front of Marlon. "You might want some sugar. It's mint. Good for slowing you down."

Marlon tried it, then added some sugar. It was warm and now sweet. Nothing wrong with it, but it also wasn't something you'd really spend money on.

"You know anyone in L.A.?" David asked.

"Not really. But I got some money in the bank. I could get a place, find a job."

"Start over," David added.

"Change my life, like you said."

"Let me ask you something," said David. He put his head down, and Marlon could see how the hair was thinning, pulling back from the forehead, just as Dirk's had, even after he started shaving it close. Suddenly David looked up.

"Have I made a difference to you?" he asked.

"What you mean?"

"Your life. Have I made it better?"

"Sure," Marlon said. It was an odd question. Marlon could never figure out why this guy cared. But it was true, he'd made a difference. Marlon had been studying him. He was quiet, and seemed comfortable alone. He was a lawyer and he had money, so Marlon figured this was proof that you could do better bending the law than breaking it.

David seemed to enjoy teaching, and so Marlon picked up bits and pieces of civilian knowledge. He could go all sorts of places now—the bank, restaurants with white people— and hardly feel out of place. The world was getting bigger by degrees. "You're helping," he told David. "For sure."

"Good enough for me," David said. "I'm going to bed."

VI

HE WENT TO work dutifully, helping Detroiters plan for death. Most of the clients lived in the suburbs, but David didn't make the distinction, the way they did. They were all Detroiters to him, just as they would all be dead. There was a wonderful equality to it. The only thing he couldn't abide was the death of the young, but the young were never his clients. The young didn't plan to die, and that was fine with David.

He needed Tiger tickets, so he walked into Bergen's office for advice. Bergen was on the phone but waved him in. Out the window was a beautiful day, the sky a royal blue with white stripes of wispy clouds. Below David could make out trees along some of the streets, coming alight with green leaves, and he couldn't help but feel his spirits lift. It was spring and he was going to a baseball game.

Bergen hung up the phone. "You're hitting the cover off the ball," Bergen said.

"How's that?"

"You billed two hundred and seventeen hours in March?"

"Sounds right."

"Look, you keep this thing going, you can hire another lawyer. Hell, we'll have a whole trust department."

David had never seen Bergen quite so animated. He mentioned his need for tickets.

"Got a buddy who knows one of Illitch's kids," Bergen said. "I'll get you set up. What game?"

"Any game."

"Pick one," Bergen said. "Don't be afraid to ask for what you want."

•   •   •

HE ALWAYS FELT a jolt when he walked into a stadium and saw the green of the field. Bergen had given him tickets for box seats along the third base side, close to the Tigers' dugout. Russell Wilson was smiling as though he'd won the lotto. "You spend a fortune?" Wilson asked. "Or are you hooked up?"

"I know someone who's hooked up."

"Same thing," said Wilson.

Over the outfield bleachers David could see the buildings of downtown Detroit, a skyline that appeared prosperous. There was some beautiful architecture right outside the stadium. By the fifth inning David had dropped seventy bucks on hot dogs and beer. The sky had turned dark, and only half of those downtown buildings had lights on. He turned his attention back to the food. Wilson said that anything eaten in a box seat tasted as good as a meal at the London Chop House, and David thought there was truth to this. The common pleasures were usually the best pleasures, in spite of what he'd often been led to believe.

David missed the old Tiger Stadium, but not because it was better. He just wanted to be young again. Still, no one here was sitting behind a steel girder. There was plenty of room to come and go. One had the sense of progress. Also, David thought this might have been the first time in his life he was out socially with a black person. It was a funny idea, really. He'd grown up in Detroit, not, say, in Alabama; he'd lived in Seattle and Denver, places he'd thought of as reasonable about race, if not entirely enlightened. But the truth was that the Detroit he'd known had been as segregated as Johannesburg, and it wasn't much different now.

"Mind if I ask you an odd question?" It was between the sixth and seventh. The Tigers, three-quarters Hispanic, were warming up.

"Do I have to answer it?" said the judge.

"Do you have any white friends?"

"A couple," he said. "I know plenty of white folk, though. I worked in the courts."

"You'd think by now—" David started to say.

"No, you wouldn't, David. You really wouldn't."

"Why not?"

"Because you wouldn't."

. . .

THE TIGERS WON. Afterward, the mood on the street was buoyant as the fans walked to their cars. The air was still warm, a hint of the summer at hand. David and Wilson walked shoulder-to-shoulder with everyone else. In this street black mixed with white.

"What happened to you?" Wilson asked.

"What do you mean?"

"A Jewish boy doesn't move from Denver back to Palmer Woods, where there are no Jews left, just on a whim. Something happened. You're fleeing disbarment, an embezzlement charge, tax evasion, something."

"I lost my son."

"Lost? Lost, as in died?"

David nodded.

Wilson stopped walking. "Marlon Booker won't change that."

"I know."

"I don't know that you do," Wilson said.

. . .

HE DROPPED WILSON at his door. Wilson thanked him and got out of the car. David pulled into his own garage, but

Wilson had come back across the strip of lawn that separated the two properties.

"What is it?" David asked.

"You know, when Dirk died and Shelly put the house up for sale, I was worried what would happen, who would move in. So I just want to say what I think you understand: I'm glad you're my neighbor."

David thanked him. There wasn't much more you could say to that, so David headed into his house. He thought that if your neighbors wanted you around, then maybe you were home.

VII

How to be a good mother: that was the question. She vowed that she would do better with this child than she'd done till now with Kevin, that she would concern herself less with progress and maturation and more with listening to him, whoever he would be. She would relax. She didn't have to prove anything to anyone.

Kevin came home from school wanting to sleep over at Bruce Silsby's house on Saturday. Carolyn had never heard of this boy, and so she called the mother, whose name was Helen, to talk about the logistics.

"It might have been nice if Bruce had told me," said

Helen Silsby, "but it's fine. We'll be here." Then she added, "Kevin seems to be adjusting quite well."

"I think so." It always spooked Carolyn when a complete stranger knew her son.

"I heard Bruce talking with another boy about him. The California Kid, they call him."

"I guess it fits," Carolyn admitted, though it was still odd to say. In Michigan, she'd noticed, no one asked you where you were from. If you were here, you hadn't come from someplace else.

She set a time with Helen Silsby. Then she called David and told him she was free.

VIII

MARLON KEPT A small tire iron under the driver's seat. It was for protection—no one needed tire irons anymore to change tires—and for what he would use it for now. He entered the house through the side door, carefully closing it, listening. There was just the sound of the heat, which still kicked on at night, the old furnace rumbling like the start of an earthquake.

Inside his room he carefully moved his bed and then used the tire iron to lift the floorboards. There it was, almost four hundred $100 bills, stacked into piles of thirty and bundled with rubber bands. He fit some of it in the bottom of his suitcase, some in a duffel bag, a third stash in his backpack. E-Call had taught him this: when thieves found a bag of money, they usually thought they had it all. "You separate," he said, " 'cause shit goes down."

He packed the clothes he thought he'd need, leaving winter stuff behind, trying to make it seem like he'd be back, though he decided to take the black pants, white shirt, black vest, and tie he wore at the bar. He replaced the floorboards and carried the three bags out to his car. It was a 1995 Escort, a little blue thing with a spoiler he'd picked up at a used car lot by paying cash. He spread the bags around as best he could. He wrapped up about ten grand in a couple T-shirts and stored it in the spare-tire well, along with the little mule that he'd never used. It occurred to him that he should leave something for David. He understood there was no way to repay him, and that, amazingly, David didn't expect to be repaid. He just did what he did, and Marlon decided that someday he would do something like that and this would be the true way he paid David back. But for now some gesture was required, so he grabbed a bundle of bills from the wheel well, three G's. He locked the car and went back inside.

It was moving on to four. He didn't want David to know right away that he was gone, and so he had to find a hiding place for the cash. He settled on the freezer—*Cold cash*, he thought—and hid the money behind a stack of Lean Cuisine frozen dinners he found there. That was really the final piece. His heart was starting to race. He was making his break. In three or four days he'd be a new man in the sunshine. It occurred to him he'd need a new name, but that was easy enough. He just needed to think one up, and there would be thousands of miles for that.

In his room he looked things over and collected the $1805 he'd saved up from the bar. This he would give to his mother. He knew she wouldn't want the drug money, but this eighteen hundred bucks he'd earned the honest way and she lived just off I-94. He had to take 94 to get to 80, which would take him all the way to Nebraska, where he'd pick up 76 down to 70. From there you drove to Utah and took 15 all the way to L.A. He'd memorized the route, as well as the names of many of the towns along the way, and not just Chicago and Denver and Las Vegas but DeKalb and Des Moines, Ogallala and St. George, Mesquite and Barstow. Places he'd never seen, or could even imagine.

He went to the kitchen for mint tea. He thought it might slow his heart. He wished he could wait until he knew Elvis was no longer after him, but with Monique seeing him, it was only a matter of time until they came to the bar. He'd heard of guys getting killed for a lot less than forty grand. Seen it, too, one junkie trying to rip and run and getting shot by E-Call before he got ten feet. Then E-Call walked up and shot him in the head while he was still alive. They left the body there, then drove down to the river and threw the gun in. "You can't let that happen," E-Call had explained. "It was him or me." This scared Marlon, because when it came to "him or me," he worried that he still wouldn't be able to pull the trigger. He was in the wrong line of work. Below them, the water sloshed by, greenish and roiling. Marlon imagined the gun on the bottom of the river, stuck in the mud on the American side.

For weeks after, he kept waiting for the police to come around asking questions, but they never did. This almost made it worse. He couldn't help but notice that life ended quickly, at any moment. A shot, a gun dropped in the river, and no one came looking for you. You just disappeared, like time itself.

Marlon found a legal pad on the table. He tore off a sheet and wrote a note. He stuck it in some dishes so it would take David at least a few days to find it, and then he headed outside.

There was dew on the grass—he could feel it making his shoes wet—and then he got to his car and heard a voice call his name. A low voice. Elvis. Immediately, before even he turned around, he felt himself change, as if the inside of him had just collapsed and yet he was still standing there, an empty shell. He shivered; he was freezing. He thought, *I'm so close. So damn close.* He made himself turn.

It wasn't Elvis. It was the old guy who lived next door, Mr. Wilson, the retired judge who seemed to have forgotten he was retired. A real busybody. He was standing in the shadow thrown by the outside garage lights, which he never turned off.

"Packing out?" he asked.

"Taking some stuff to my mom." He had thought he was going to die.

"Awful early."

"She lives out in Ypsi," Marlon said. "Works early."

"You're not stealing anything from David, now, are you?"

"No, sir. I'd never. I ain't no thief."

The judge eyed him in the darkness. Marlon had the feeling Wilson wanted to frisk him.

"You realize what that man has done for you?" Wilson asked.

"Sure." Marlon's mouth was so dry he could barely get the word out.

"No, I don't think you do. But someday you might."

The judge turned and walked back to his house. Marlon was still damp with fear. He had sweated through his shirt, and, worse, he'd pissed himself. It was dark and he didn't think the judge had seen it. He thought he heard something and he stopped again, his soaked pants clinging to his thighs. He took a breath and held the air down in his lungs. Through the quiet he heard a bird, then two of them, announcing the dawn.

IX

RUSSELL WILSON WAS waiting for him when he got home, standing at the edge of the driveway in that tracksuit. "Sorry I missed you this morning," he said, "but I think Marlon took off today. You better check the house."

"Check the house for what?" David asked.

"Anything missing."

David invited him in, but Wilson said he'd stay on the lawn. Inside everything seemed normal. David had some cash he kept in his sock drawer along with his passport, but both were still there. Only Marlon's room looked different. Clothes still hung in the closet and there were a few things in the drawers, but it looked emptier than the last time David had been here. There was no extra pair of sneakers on the floor, no baseball caps on the one chair, no dirty clothes on the floor. Still, David couldn't believe Marlon would just leave like that, without even a goodbye. There had to be some reasonable explanation.

As David walked from the closet, he tripped over something and had to put his hand down on the bed. He found a small tire iron on the floor. Odd, he thought.

Outside, in the sunshine, he told Wilson everything was in order, though it also seemed possible that Marlon was gone.

"You aren't happy about that?" Wilson asked.

"No. I like the kid."

Wilson shook his head.

"I can't believe he didn't say goodbye," David said.

"You go back inside, you look for the thing that has the most value to you, and you make sure it's there. Then you have the locks changed and count your blessings."

David went back in. He knew nothing was missing, but to be sure, he checked the bookshelf for the letters he'd written to Cory. They were still there. He sat down to write another.

X

CAROLYN HAD BIG plans for the evening, but by the time she got to David's she didn't feel like going out. Pregnancy had a way of doing that.

"But I made reservations at the Wendy's on Livernois," David said. When she smiled at him, he said, "Would you believe Joe Muer's?" Even she knew it had been torn down. In fact, he'd made reservations at an Italian place. He called to cancel and then went to put a frozen pizza in the oven. Even before it was baked she was so tired she could barely speak. She asked him to do the talking. "Tell me something about you I don't know," she said, and that's when she got the full story of his lost son, of the fight and the yelling and the slap and the permanent inability to make it right. She learned that he wrote the dead boy letters, even though there was no place to send them. She found it sad and beautiful and somehow comforting.

•   •   •

SOON THEY WERE heading upstairs. She had asked for this. "Will you sleep with me but not sleep with me?" was how she'd put it. She was too tired for sex, too big, too . . . unsexy. But if he would lie beside her and hold her and sleep with her through the night, then she would be happy.

As she walked into the bedroom, she saw a piece of metal on the bed.

"It's a tire iron," David explained. "Marlon left it behind."

"Why's it here?"

"I figure I can use it for protection," he said.

"Why not get a gun?"

"God, if I had a gun, I'd probably get depressed and shoot myself."

"See, David," she said, "that's the difference between you and me. If I had a gun, I'd probably get depressed and shoot someone else."

• • •

SHE SLEPT WELL, but then woke to pee. Afterward, she couldn't get back to sleep. It was about half past midnight. She decided to go downstairs and make some tea. That was one thing she knew about David: he had tea. She thought again about him writing letters to his dead son. It was a bizarre thing to do, but she didn't mind that he was doing it. He'd lost a son, and you had to allow him a little craziness.

XI

HE HEARD PEOPLE downstairs. He opened his eyes and saw darkness, didn't know where he was, and then recognized the ceiling, his room, the new one. He reached over for Carolyn, but the bed was empty.

He rose, put on his robe. It was a little after one according to the green light of his alarm clock. He thought he heard walking, boots on the hardwood floors. Marlon, perhaps, come back with friends. Or maybe just Carolyn. He walked to the stairs and called down to her.

"Don't come down!" came the reply, her voice so distraught, so panicked, that it created the same feelings in him: he felt his bowels slacken and sweat form on the back of his neck.

"Get down here," said a voice. Low, male, black.

David stopped, turned, went back to the bedroom for the tire iron. It was cold in his hand, and it occurred to him that he'd fetched it without thought, as if the instinct to have a weapon were simply inside him. Now he wished he'd gotten a gun, not that he'd ever fired one. He'd grown up in the suburbs. As for tire irons, he'd used one once, when Carter was president, to change a tire.

There were footsteps, boots on the stairs, heavy weight ascending. Every molecule in David's body wanted to flee, to hide, but Carolyn was down there. He thought he could hear her sobbing. He moved down the hallway toward the stairs, the footsteps nearing, the pace methodical, a metronome. The first thing he saw was the gun, and then, briefly, a man, shaved head, leather jacket, but by the time this registered David was already swinging. The tire iron hit the man in the forehead with a damp clang. The bar vibrated in David's hands. There was a brief moment—probably less than a second, though it seemed far longer—when time stopped; David saw surprise, pain, then blankness pass across the man's face, and then the world spun again and the man fell backward, banging and crashing down the stairs. The gun, though, fell onto the second-floor landing, bounced twice on the wood, and came to rest on the runner that ran the length of the hallway.

David peeked down the stairs. The man—even from here he looked huge—lay sprawled at the bottom of the stairs. It was so quiet that for a second David thought he'd gone deaf, but then the voice came back.

"Get down here, or she's dead."

"Don't come down," Carolyn yelled.

They hit her. David heard it, and then he heard her cry.

"I'm going to give you one minute to be down here, or she's dead."

He was sure they meant it.

"I'm coming," he called.

David took the gun. It was surprisingly heavy. Somewhere, he thought, there was a safety. He didn't know where, but he knew that much. Probably it was off. The man at the bottom of the stairs would have come up armed.

He would trade his life for hers. Just as he would have traded his life for Cory's. Here it was: the great second chance of his life. There was one goal now, to get her out. He took a breath and started down. He could see the body below him. He looked at the grain of the stained wood on the stairs and was struck by its beauty, surprised that he'd never noticed it before. He took in the smell of the house, a faint, dry odor, perhaps from the old books. He looked again at the man at the bottom of the stairs. He descended with confidence. Now that he had decided to give up his own life, he felt invincible.

Two steps from the bottom of the stairs he saw them. Carolyn was in his reading chair. A man stood in front of her pointing a gun at her head. She was quietly sobbing. The man holding the gun was tall and lean, expressionless, also in a leather jacket. Beside him was the kid who had come with Marlon to David's office the day they met.

David stepped over the man at the bottom of the stairs.

"Drop the gun or I'll blow her brains out."

David considered. "And then I'll kill you," he said. His voice sounded very loud in his head. Slowly he raised the gun, sighted it as best he could. He held it with two hands, the way he'd seen police do it on TV. The man was maybe twenty feet away, close enough, he thought, for him to feel uncertain about his chances.

The man nodded to the kid, Marlon's friend. The kid produced a gun from his waistband and pointed it at David.

"Two beats one," said the man.

"What do you want?" David asked.

No one said anything. He looked at Carolyn. Her head was down, her hair hanging snarled over her face. She sniffled. Gasped.

"Marlon. You give me Marlon and you live."

"Why should I trust you?" David said.

"Don't," Carolyn cried.

With his free hand, the man slapped her. She cried out. David moved forward.

"You got no choice," said the man. David stood perfectly still, trying to think his way through this. The man stepped away from Carolyn and said, "E, shoot the bitch."

David squeezed the trigger. He was pointing the gun at the man, but nothing happened. He pulled harder and still nothing happened. A long, agonizing second passed. He charged, ran right at the man, who was still pointing the gun at him. Later, the utter foolishness of this act was apparent, but at the moment he was merely running, throwing himself into the fray, trying to stop what couldn't be stopped.

The explosion so startled him that he fell to his knees. For a moment he thought he'd been shot, but he felt nothing. Carolyn screamed. That was when he knew she was okay. David lay facedown on the floor. He looked up and there in front of him was the man, eyes blank, head bleeding. It was eerie, chilling. David had never before looked into a dead man's eyes. He crawled around the man to Carolyn.

She was on the floor, sobbing. He held her and then looked up at the kid, who almost smiled. Then he set his gun on the floor; a tendril of smoke rose from its barrel. He stood and put his palms up.

"That's all," he said. "It's over."

XII

HE WALKED OVER to check on Dre; the man was dead. He had a big bump on the front of his head, and whether the blow had killed him or the cartwheels down the stairs, E-Call couldn't say. He was just glad, 'cause you didn't shoot Elvis and not expect Dre to do something about it.

He looked back at the man and the pregnant lady. The whole thing was fucked up. He knew Elvis was after Marlon, but till tonight, when they found what must have been the hiding place in the floor joists, he hadn't really believed that Marlon was skimming. He just thought that Elvis had the wrong impression. Of course, when a man had an impression and a gun, the truth wasn't all that important. Marlon had split, and that was smart, but it was sad, too, because E-Call wasn't sure he'd ever see him again. Marlon was really the only family he had. More family than his own real brother.

The lawyer was moving the woman away from Elvis. E-Call felt relief at his death, and so he knew he'd made the right decision. And he'd made that decision early, as soon as they got in the house, because Elvis never brought E-Call along for things like this. He was a street seller, all retail, not muscle, so Elvis must have had an impression. He must have wanted to keep an eye on him. There was probably someone back at E-Call's place right now, looking for the lost cash. Marlon had told him to get out, and that was right. Now, especially, he'd have to disappear, which was easy enough. He'd planned for it.

They all went to the kitchen. "Why? Why'd you do that?" the lawyer asked. He handed E-Call a Vernor's, which was good. E-Call liked Vernor's, and his mouth was very dry.

"Why you do it? You thought you was gonna run through a bullet."

"I had to do something."

"Like die?"

"I wasn't thinking about myself."

"Well, I was," E-Call said. "And I was next. When you took care of Dre, you made it easy. And besides, it wasn't right, hitting a pregnant lady. There are supposed to be rules."

"Thank you," the woman said.

"You welcome." He took a swig of Vernor's. Nothing ever had tasted so good. "Mostly I did it for Marlon."

"Do you know what happened to him?"

"He gone. That was the smart play, and Marlon was always smart."

"Did he really take money from those men?" the lawyer asked.

"I bet he did. He was a man with a plan. I just did my part, you know. For Marlon."

"For Marlon?"

"We family. Can't be nothing that trumps that."

"Family?" the lawyer asked.

"Came up together," E-Call told him, feeling nostalgic, wishing Marlon were here. "Thicker than blood."

XIII

RUSSELL WILSON CAME in with the police. He knew the lead detective. They left Carolyn in the kitchen with the paramedics and they sat David down in the dining room and asked him questions. He kept two secrets. First, that the "robbers" had been after Marlon. Second, who the kid was who turned on his boss. The detective told David he was one lucky SOB, and David didn't argue.

The detective, who was black, folded up his notebook and took another moment to think on the matter. "Just one more question," he said. "What are you doing here?"

"What do you mean?"

"Here. In Palmer Woods. I mean, you just moved in, right?"

And that's when Wilson piped up from the side of the room. David hadn't even known he was still there.

"He belongs here," Wilson said.

The detective looked at the judge, then back at David, and left without speaking.

•   •   •

TWO NIGHTS LATER he took Kevin to a Tigers game.

It was Carolyn's idea. She thought they needed to spend time together, and David could see her point. David hadn't formed an opinion of the kid one way or the other. He was quiet, that was all. David had gone back to Bergen and asked for two good seats. They again ended up just behind the Tigers' dugout.

For two innings David got nothing but one-word answers. Then, in the third, Kevin turned to him. "You know," he said, "you're not my dad."

"I know that. And I don't want to be."

"Then what are you doing here?"

"I happen to be in love with your mother. I'd like us all to make a home together. But no one will ever be your father except your father."

"You can't boss me around," the kid said.

"You listen to your mother, that's good enough for me."

Kevin looked at the field and David said, "You miss your dad?"

The boy turned, and David thought he saw the kid relax. He'd been rigid, trying to stand against David, fighting some battle he probably didn't understand. "Yeah," Kevin said. "I guess. A little."

"I get that."

"What do you get?"

"I know what it is to miss someone," David said. "I miss my son."

XIV

THE BLACK DETECTIVE had been back to see them twice. He had it pretty well figured out. He knew about Marlon Booker.

"It had to have been a drug dispute," the detective said. They were sitting in the living room, the scene of the crime, though cleaned up now. It was odd, Carolyn thought, how surviving that night had made the room hers. At least, that's how she thought about it.

The detective's name was Cousins. "They tore up that room where this Marlon Booker stayed. They were after something."

Carolyn nodded.

"Did you understand," the detective asked David, "that you were letting a drug criminal stay in your home?"

"He'd gone straight," David said. "He had a legitimate job."

Detective Cousins rubbed his forehead, then shook his head. "But why this kid?"

"He was my brother's nephew," Carolyn said. "This used to be my brother's house. We felt we needed to help the boy."

"That's the other thing," Cousins said. "The deceased, Charles Werther, aka Elvis, and Andre Cassidy? We think there's a connection to your brother's and sister's shooting." He explained that circumstantial evidence existed. "We found a newspaper clipping of the story at

Cassidy's apartment, and there's a street camera shot of Mr. Burton's car being followed by Cassidy's car. But we don't have any solid proof, and we can't find a motive. Agent Burton was long retired, and he had no connection to these two when he was at the FBI. It really doesn't make any sense, except for this: they both knew Marlon Booker."

"But why would that make them want to kill Dirk and Natalie?" David asked.

"What makes sense to men like that doesn't always make sense to you or me. But Booker has run, so he must have known he was being hunted. Werther and Cassidy ended up here looking for him. The car Mr. Burton and Ms. Brooks were killed in was registered to this address. You don't have to be a genius to know that their killing was related to Booker."

Like the detective, Carolyn had guessed that Marlon might have had something to do with Natalie's death. It would have been nice to know exactly how and why, but she realized she wasn't going to get that kind of answer. Dirk had always cared for Marlon, and it had got him and Natalie killed. It was a terrible price for doing the right thing.

"What about the shooter here?" David asked.

"Oh," said the detective, "I think I know who that was. Process of elimination. But he's in the wind."

"Can you find him?" Carolyn asked. She wanted the kid to get away. He had saved their lives. He deserved his freedom.

"We will," Cousins said, "but he did the world a bit of a favor. I, for one, am willing to go easy on that kid. These guys, Werther and Cassidy, were the scum of the earth." He closed his notebook. "Sometimes—not often, but sometimes—it's funny how things can work out."

XV

A STRAY DOG kept coming to the back yard for food till he let it move in. It had tags. Champ was its name. David called the owners, but the number had been disconnected. Champ was some kind of hound mix, content to sleep at David's feet and howl whenever someone or something (a heavy wind, say) passed by the house. The dog had adopted this home, and David felt safer for it.

He'd been thinking about what Judge Wilson had told him about Marlon, that trouble followed the boy. The judge had been right. Still, David didn't regret helping Marlon. He felt proud of it. He understood why Dirk had worked so hard for the kid: there was something there worth saving, and when you saw that, what choice did you really have? Still, the consequences were unpredictable. David had been lucky, and Dirk had not. David hoped that Marlon was out in the world reinventing himself, and that someday they would meet again, but not too soon.

• • •

HE'D BEEN THINKING about changing out his car. His new life demanded something different, and it was the dog that put him over. Champ just didn't belong in an Audi. He soon found himself at a Ford dealership just north of 8 Mile. He parked the Audi by the entrance, so that it could easily be seen from the showroom. A salesman came up to him as soon as he walked in. He was a short white man in a three-piece suit. David hadn't seen anyone wear a three-piece suit since the last time he'd lived in Detroit.

"May I help you, sir?" the salesman asked.

"Yeah. I want to trade in that Audi for an American car. Am I in the right place?"

"God bless you, sir."

He found himself looking at the modern version of the station wagon, a midsize SUV, with its backseat bench and storage behind. He resisted the idea, but he had a lot of chattel now and he needed a car to hold it. It didn't take long to make a deal.

"What brings you here from Colorado?" asked the salesman. David still hadn't changed his plates.

"I'm moving back home. Thought I should drive something American."

"Consider yourself home," the man said.

XVI

SHE NAMED HIM Karl, with a K, after his great-grandfather who died in the war. He was eight pounds, seven ounces, and beautiful, with a shock of dark hair and brown eyes he almost never opened. He slept, he ate, he rarely cried: a contented baby, so unlike Kevin at the beginning, who cried every minute he wasn't sucking and who was bald with just some corn-colored fuzz.

And he came quickly, two weeks early and just five hours after her water broke. Amazingly, she'd forgotten the agony of labor, but she held David's hand and screamed. When it was over, they cleaned her up and then she held the little boy. At that moment she felt her heart slow; she was exhausted. She looked at him and then closed her eyes as his were closed and held him to her chest.

It was three in the morning. The next afternoon she took the baby home to David's. It was her home, something she'd fought for. It proved she was stronger than she'd thought. Kevin, too, had gone along with the move.

One day, about two weeks into Karl's life, David came to her while she was nursing. "We need to go see my father," he said. "I haven't had a chance to tell him yet."

. . .

THEY DIDN'T CALL. They loaded everyone in the car, then drove north to the suburbs, dropped Kevin at a friend's, and headed to Sol's. David said the old man would be there, and he was, wearing a pair of jeans pulled up as high as his belly button.

"Let's go to the living room," David said.

They walked to the living room and Carolyn and David sat on the couch. Karl slept in the little carrier that snapped into the holder in her car and became a car seat. In front of her was a table littered with old papers and used coffee cups.

"So, Dad, here's what we came to say: this baby, I'm the father. Carolyn is the mother. And you, Dad, you're the grandfather."

Sol was in the reading chair to Carolyn's left. Karl was in his carrier. She reached out and lifted Karl slowly, then placed him on the floor by Sol. The baby slept, didn't so much as take a deeper breath.

"This is Karl," she said.

She expected that he might be angry—why, he might have asked, didn't you tell me?—but he seemed perfectly calm. He reached out and lightly touched the handle to Karl's carrier. "You two have given me reason to get out of bed in the morning," he told them.

He smiled at her, and Carolyn wished her own father could have shared this moment. He'd been gone for years. Long stretches went by when she did not think of him, and then suddenly the loss of him hurt sharply, as it did now. She wished Dirk and Natalie could be here, too. It was a pity; almost no one had gotten through.

XVII

The clouds had burned off. He drove south, the radio playing "What I Like About You," one of the anthems of his high school years. They all were headed back down the Lodge Expressway. At 7 Mile he looked left, as if he could see his home. Next they passed the exit for the art museum and then, a little beyond, the spot where Dirk and Natalie had died. He drove faster. There was a new casino, of all things, to the right as they continued south. Detroit was a city where you could be right downtown and still drive your car at seventy-five miles per hour.

He parked at the Ren Cen, then led Carolyn and Kevin up to the esplanade along the river. He carried his sleeping son in his right arm. Kevin moved out ahead, pulled along by Champ. They strolled along the water without speaking. Everyone seemed to be enjoying the sun and the fine warm weather, not the way people took it for granted in Denver. The river reflected the sun, as did the windows of Windsor across the way.

"What are you thinking?" Carolyn asked.

"That we have a second chance."

"You know, you can call anything a second chance."

"Thank God for that," he said.

She smiled at him, and then Karl began to fuss. "I'm sure he's hungry by now," she said. David handed him back and checked on Kevin, who was walking Champ around them in big circles. David was again reminded how a young child's needs were immediate; it kept you living close to the ground, focused on the true moments. They found a bench in the sun and Carolyn fed Karl, covered by a light blanket, as Detroiters walked up and down the riverfront.

He looked at Carolyn, then at his son, the little feet sticking out from the blanket, and then at his stepson. He had responsibilities now, and he intended to enjoy them. He and Carolyn had talked of moving out of the city, but in the end they'd found each other here.

A year ago he couldn't have imagined he'd ever come back, and now he couldn't fathom leaving. His old friends, on the other hand, had all scattered. Still, he knew that Tom Phillips and Tim Forrester weren't so different from him, that they'd get curious and then one day he'd get a call. They'd want to know where he was, and he would relish their surprise when he told them he had stayed.

Acknowledgments

FOR VITAL HELP and support in the writing of this book, I am indebted to James Watkins, Liz Duvall, Alison Liss, Emerald Cousin, Jennifer Barron, and especially Derek Green, Pamela Bowen Stanley, Jill Bialosky, and Jennifer Rudolph Walsh.

SAY NICE THINGS ABOUT DETROIT

Scott Lasser

SAY NICE THINGS
ABOUT DETROIT

Scott Lasser

AUTHOR'S NOTE

One day in my youth I went over to my girlfriend's house, and in the driveway I found a souped-up Mercedes with dual-chrome exhaust, twenty-inch back wheels, and rear-mounted speakers behind darkly tinted windows. A drug-dealer car, out of place in this neighborhood. And then my blonde girlfriend walked out of the house with a tall black man whom she introduced as her brother. I didn't even know she had a brother. Besides, this was Detroit, one of the most segregated cities in the country, where blonde girls didn't tend to have black brothers, or vice versa (these two shared the same mother). I thought, *Wow, there's an awful lot in the world I don't know about. I really need to write about this.*

And so I finally have.

I got started on this book in 2008. It was several months before Lehman Brothers (my former employer, as it turns out) would go under and almost take the world economy with it, but no one was really feeling it yet. Except in Detroit.

Sometimes numbers can tell a story; in Detroit the statistics are mind-boggling. The city has lost so many people that those who have left outnumber all the people who currently live in San Francisco. The open space inside Detroit's borders, taken as a whole, is greater than the entire area of Boston. The 2010 census showed that in the first decade of this millennium Detroit lost a quarter of its citizens, or 100,000 more people than New Orleans without a Katrina.

I knew I had to set a novel in Detroit.

The city was already losing population when I was born there, but I was raised to feel great pride in my hometown. In its heyday Detroit was the seat of America's industrial might—"the arsenal of democracy," FDR called it—and arguably the world's most powerful engine of wealth creation. It is the birthplace of the American middle class. Its contributions to American music are inestimable. And it is largely a ruin.

So, how to tackle this in a novel? I decided early on that I wanted to model my story on that most classic of human tales: the journey home. After all, we're talking about Detroit. Damn near everyone has already left.

All I needed was a way in, and then I remembered that girl-friend and her brother.

I should add that the Mercedes was, in fact, a drug-dealer car. The brother was an FBI agent, and he was using that car for his undercover work. This incident, fictionalized, makes up the first couple pages of *Say Nice Things About Detroit*. It gave me entrée into the story of race, family, home, and dreams gone awry and reimagined that you find here.

DISCUSSION QUESTIONS

1. Detroit is more than background for the novel—it plays an essential role in the story and in the hearts and minds of the characters. What are some of the landmarks and scenes that help bring the city to life?

2. Everett and Dirk love each other like brothers. David comes, briefly, to think of Marlon as a son. How do the characters in the novel construct and experience family?

3. The Detroit that the novel shows us is deeply segregated, but some of the characters in the novel—Dirk, Natalie, David—are able to transcend the boundaries of race. What are some of the challenges they face in doing so, and how do they overcome those challenges?

4. David and Dirk never meet, but their connection runs deep: David falls in love with Dirk's half-sister, he buys Dirk's old house, and he cares for Dirk's nephew. Does David feel he has inherited a kind of legacy from Dirk? What kind of a legacy?

5. The novel begins just after the murder of Dirk and Natalie, and it ends just after the attempted murder of David and Carolyn. In what ways do these two crime scenes mirror each other? What has changed, from beginning to end, and what, do we suspect, will always remain the same?

6. The novel's title comes from a slogan on a child's T-shirt (p. 60). How does the title reflect and comment on the characters' relationship with their city?

7. Many of the characters in the novel are parents of young sons. What do some of these parent-child relationships have in common? How do they differ?

8. In the end, the reader knows something that the characters never will: how and why Dirk and Natalie were killed. Why do you think the author chose to reveal this information to the reader but not to David or Carolyn? What is the effect?

9. David and Carolyn start a new family and a new life in a familiar place, honoring the past as they move into the future. In what ways will Cory, Dirk, and Natalie remain with them?

10. Carolyn watches her son meet up with his friends at the same fast-food joint she used to go to as a girl. David takes a neighbor to see his favorite childhood baseball team play, but at a new stadium. What does it mean to go home again? Is it possible?

Manil Suri   *The Age of Shiva*
Brady Udall   *The Lonely Polygamist*
Barry Unsworth   *Sacred Hunger*
Alexei Zentner   *Touch*

*Available only on the Norton Web site